DAUGHTER OF A THUG, WIFE OF A GANGSTA

A Thug Legacy Story

MZ. LADY P

Shan Presents, LLC

NOV 2019

FR

SUBSCRIBE

Text Shan to 22828 to stay up to date with new releases, sneak peeks, contest, and more....

WANT TO BE A PART OF SHAN PRESENTS?

To submit your manuscript to Shan Presents, please send the first three chapters and synopsis to submissions@shanpresents.com

Chapter One

YAH-YAH

One Year Later

Over the years, I've watched my parent's drama unfold before my siblings and me. I always said I would never allow a man to treat me the way my father did my mother. He treated her like a queen, but he also hurt her from time to time. Growing up, I promised myself that I would never sit around and just allow it to happen like she did. Now, don't get me wrong. My mother didn't take shit from him easily. I just never understood why she stayed. Now that I'm an adult, I'm glad she did because it made our family stronger. Watching her go through certain things, I always vowed never to let that happen to me.

It's been a year since we had our son Yahmeen Jr. For the longest, I've always told his ass never to put the streets ahead of us, but he just keeps on doing it, and I'm fed up. I'm too fucking young and beautiful to be dealing with this type of bullshit from him.

For the third night this week, he's let the sun beat him home. That shit is disrespectful, and I'm not taking any types of disrespect from his ass. If you let a nigga slide, the bitch is gone think he can ice skate. He got me completely fucked up, and he's going to learn today.

Since my son was asleep, I flamed up the fattest blunt ever. A bitch needed to get high to deal with the bullshit that was going on. At any second, he was going to be pulling up, but he wasn't even ready for the surprise waiting on him.

❧

"Come on, Yah-Yah! Open the door. You got all these nosey ass neighbors in our business. Why the fuck is all my clothes outside? And, what the fuck did my dog do to you? Fuck you put her out for?"

Yahmeen's dumb ass finally decided to come home. He was pissed off all of his shit was outside, but I didn't give a fuck.

"Fuck you and that motherfucking dog, Yahmeen! I told you if the sun ever beat your light, bright ass home, I was putting your ass out. The crazy part is that your ass has done this shit three times this week. You might as well climb in that cage with that mutt with your dog ass!"

"If you don't open this door I'm going to kick this bitch in and fuck you up!"

His nutty ass started kicking the door hard as hell, and I laughed at his ass. He forgot who the fuck I am talking about fucking me up.

"Then my daddy gone murder ya ass!"

"Your daddy's a thug, but I'm a motherfucking gangsta! I don't scare that easily! Fuck you, Yah-Yah! You're childish as hell. You're a grown ass woman who's about to be married with a son. When are you going to realize you're not some little ass girl whose father runs the city? In case you forgot, your pops is retired, and your husband is doing numbers in the streets. Since you want me gone, I'll leave. Take your spoiled ass home to your daddy. I need a wife, not a nagging ass brat." Yahmeen chucked up the deuces and hopped in his Benz.

Before I felt like I was in control, but I had quickly lost that. He wasn't supposed to walk out. He was supposed to beg for forgiveness. Then I remembered Yahmeen wasn't one of those niggas that gave in quick. He had grown so much from the teenager my father and brothers tried to scare. He and his family have become moguls in the business industry, not to mention the biggest drug traffickers since Thug Inc. My husband had more money than we knew what to do with. At twenty-one years old, we were living a life that most people never see. All of my life I've had everything so this shit is nothing to me. Since Yahmeen wants to talk that shit and bounce whenever he does return, I won't be here. I'm going home to my parents.

§.

"I don't fucking think so! I love you and my grandbaby, but you can't stay here. Go home to that big ass mansion you live in. If my first house were that damn big when I married your daddy, I would have never left."

I rolled my eyes at my mother as she walked around in a red silk kimono and red bottoms. Boss Lady still is the flyest chick on the scene.

"What's that supposed to mean? You had the biggest house on the block."

"I know, babe. I'm just saying Yah-Yah's first house was bigger than my first house. That's all."

My mother sashayed her fast ass over to my daddy and kissed him so passionately. These two just can't seem to keep their hands off each other. As I stood and watched them, I realized I wanted that type of life with Yahmeen.

"You got to go home, Yah-Yah."

Tears welled up in my eyes because my daddy's face showed me he meant that shit. I'm still so spoiled, and I hate when he tells me no.

"Really daddy? Yahmeen's not acting right, and I don't know what else to do."

"As a wife, it's your job to get him to act right. Crying, nagging, and being a brat won't get you any results," my mother said as she sipped from her glass of wine.

"Then what am I supposed to do?"

"Shoot him in the ass! If nothing makes a nigga act right, a bullet most definitely will. Ain't that right, baby?" She winked at my daddy.

"Hell yeah. My ass still hurts from time to time!" My daddy rubbed his ass as he and mother started hugging and kissing again. If they aren't dysfunctional, I don't know what is.

I sat and continued to contemplate my next move. At that

moment, I knew I had to stand up in the paint if I really wanted to be Yahmeen's wife. He better straighten the fuck up before I have to result to shooting him in the ass. If my momma could straighten out my daddy, I could definitely straighten out Yahmeen.

Chapter Two

YAHMEEN

It had been hours since I left home, and I missed Yah-Yah's nutty ass already. That girl had a nigga's heart in her pocket, and she had no idea. The thing with Yah-Yah is that she's spoiled and comes from wealth. The shit I do for her she's basically accustomed to, so it doesn't move her like that. As much as I love her that spoiled behavior is the biggest turn off for a nigga. That shit makes a nigga want to leave and never come back. I would never do no shit like that cause I love her and my son too much.

Sitting on the block, I got heated immediately looking at her car pulling up. If there was nothing I hated more, it was her being on the block. She thought that shit was so cool.

"Go home, Ka'Jaiyah!" I said before she could even pull up good enough.

"We need to talk!"

"We'll talk at home. Take my son home. Fuck I tell you about bringing him out here. You know I hate your ass on the block!" She just couldn't go home without questioning my authority. That would be too much like right on her part.

"Don't be trying to show out, Yahmeen! I'll show out right with your ass."

Instead of entertaining her drama, I walked away from her ass and got in my car. I refused to give the hood some shit to talk about. I have a business to run, and this shit is bad for business. Instead of heading home to our crib, I went to her parent's crib. That's where she needed to be. Of course, she was right behind me. As a matter of fact, she was weaving in and out of traffic like she was crazy. The fact that she had my son in the backseat made my decision even more of the right one. I love Yah-Yah, but this isn't working for me.

§

About thirty minutes later, we were pulling into the driveway. Before she could even fully stop the car, she was jumping out on that rah-rah shit.

"Why the fuck you pulling up to my parents' house?"

"You want to keep acting like a kid! Then this is where you need to be. Fuck wrong with you driving like that with my seed in the car!"

"What the fuck is wrong with y'all out here?"

"That's him, ma. I told you he's acting all stupid. I went over there to talk to him, and he started acting crazy! Give me my baby, Yahmeen!"

"I wish you would snatch my son out my arms!" She stood back because our son is the one thing I'm not even about to play with her about, so she could miss me with that shit.

"Fuck going on out here! Why you crying, Yah-Yah?"

Thug had now come out looking like an old school nigga in his glory. He had on a Versace robe with matching slippers. The nigga had on so much ice that I was blinded. Hell, if retirement looked like that let me get back to the block.

"Yahmeen is just being mean and stupid, daddyyy!" She was crying and really putting on a show as if I had done something to her.

"Stop all that damn crying, Ka'Jaiyah! I don't want to hear that shit. Now, what the hell is wrong with my daughter?" Ms. Tahari spoke with an attitude.

"Yah-Yah's spoiled and wants what she wants! I hate when she comes on the block with Jr. That isn't a place for my future wife and my son. She doesn't understand that though. She wants to pull up with all that loud talking, bringing too much attention to me. I'm out there getting this money so that I can provide. I can get caught lacking by an enemy like that, not to mention she can become a target and that's some shit I don't want. Yah-Yah needs to understand that she's in a relationship. I understand she was raised strong, but there is nothing I can do for Yah-Yah if she doesn't want to let me lead. I'm not trying to be disrespectful to either of you, but this is where she needs to be. There is nothing I won't do for her or my son, but until she realizes that she's a grown woman and not a kid, we can't be together."

"Are you serious right now, Yahmeen?"

"Dead ass. I'll call you later to work out some type of arrangement so that I can see my son. I'm a phone call away when you need me, or if you want to get on your grown woman shit."

It hurt me to leave her like that, but I had to. That's tough love from a hood nigga. She might not understand now, but she will later. I have to get back to my bag. I didn't even wait for her parents to say anything. What could they say? I handled that shit like the gangsta I am.

Pulling back up to the block shit was popping and in full swing.

"Where sis crazy ass go?" my brother Yasir asked when I hopped out the car.

"I dropped her ass back off to her OG 'nem. I don't have time for Yah-Yah's spoiled ass."

"Quit fronting, nigga. You know damn well you're going to get her crazy ass before you take it in."

Yasir was laughing, and I didn't see shit funny. I was so serious this time. Yah-Yah needed to start behaving like a wife of a gangsta. She needs to dead all of that spoiled rich girl shit she's been on.

"You'll see nigga. Her ass is on punishment until I'm ready to take her off." She's going to learn today who wears the pants in this relationship.

"Good luck because I'm not convinced. Yah-Yah is nutty as fuck.

Let's bow our head in prayer cause she's about to give your ass a run for your money."

I flamed up a blunt and zoned out on his ass. I was good on her crazy ass. As I smoked on the blunt, I looked around at the block and knew I wanted more. It was only so much my father, Hunan, would let me do. This nigga was one of the biggest heroin distributors the Chi had ever seen, and he was basically bird feeding Yasir and me. We do moves for him every now and then but it's not enough. Not for the lifestyle I desire for my family.

"I've been thinking we need to get our own shit going. This block shit is lucrative, but I want more."

"Pops will never let that happen. He would rather us start from the bottom instead of giving us the key to the streets.

"How about we find our own key? We don't need his permission. We know the ins and outs of this shit. All we need is his support. We can do this shit Bro."

"Yah-Yah is driving your ass crazy for real if I think you're saying what I think you're saying. I'm not trying to be at war with our father."

"I'm not trying to be at war with him either. I just want us to go to him and tell him we want more. I got big dreams, my nigga. That added with a son and future wife I have to give the world to. Granted we young and rich already, however, it's not enough. I see how that nigga Thug is living in retirement. The nigga walks around in Versace, smoking blunts, and fucking a lining out of Ms. Tahari."

"So, this is about Thug? You want to be like ya bitch's pops."

"It ain't another nigga out here in the world I want to be like. It's just that I see where Yah-Yah comes from. She's not basic period. I want to be able to provide for her while we're young and when we get old. She's bat shit crazy, but I love her, and I want to give her the world. This block shit won't get that, so I'm definitely going to holla at pops. You with me or nah?"

"Hell yeah, I'm with you. Just be prepared because he's not going to do it."

"Then we just have to do what we have to do."

"No doubt!"

We shook it up, and for the rest of the night, we chilled on the block and did a count before heading in. Yah-Yah was all I could think about as I laid in our bed. I wanted to go over to her parents' house and get her, but I couldn't. She had to know I was so serious about her respecting me as the man of the house.

The next morning, I woke up on a mission to go and talk with my father. I didn't have a nervous bone in my body as I pulled in the driveway. I was glad Yasir car was in the driveway. For a minute I thought his pussy ass was gone punk out on me, but he didn't. There were other cars in the driveway, and that surprised me. They were unfamiliar, so it piqued my interest.

Once I placed the car in park, I headed inside. I smiled the moment I stepped into the foyer. My mother, Aminah, greeted me with open arms as usual. She was the most loving and nurturing woman a kid could ever ask for. I've always felt sorry that she had to be my father's wife. She was far too angelic and pure to be with a man like him. Now don't get me wrong. I love my father, but he's true to his Saudi Arabian heritage. It was hard growing up and seeing the American way of life but living life as a Saudi Arabian family. Mind you, Yasir and I were born in Chicago, so we knew nothing about it.

For the first ten years of my life, all I knew was the importance of working. My parents owned chains of grocery stores and gas stations all over the city of Chicago. It wasn't until my thirteenth birthday I found out they were all fronts for my family's drug business. Once my father realized that both Yasir and I knew what he did, he started grooming us for the business. However, he has never given us full access. At twenty-one, I no longer feel the need for my father to bird feed me. I'm trying to get the full course meal by any means necessary.

"I'm so happy to see you, son. It would be even better if I can see my grandson more."

"I'll talk with Yah-Yah about bringing him over more often. I've been extremely busy. "Where is Yasir?"

"He's in the conference room with your father and his associates. They're actually waiting for you."

She kissed me on the jaw then quickly walked off. That was odd of her but what was even odder was that they were waiting on me. He had no idea I was coming over unless Yasir told his ass about the plan before I made it.

"Just the man we're waiting for! Come over and meet my good friend Hashib and his daughter Raja."

I shook their hands and took a seat at the table with them. Yasir wouldn't make eye contact with me, and it was pissing me off. I needed to know what the fuck was up. I didn't come here to be in a meeting with anyone else.

"What's going on?"

"Well son, this is my business partner, and I think it's time you get to meet him. Soon, I'll be stepping down and giving all of this to your brother and you. Hashib has no boys, and Raja is his only daughter. He will only step down and give his portion to Raja if she is a married woman, which is why she's come to the United States. I've decided you will marry her and keep this legacy going."

I had to look hard at this crazy motherfucker. He had lost his mind trying to marry me off like I was his property or something. I'm a whole nigga out here. I don't give a fuck what dude got going on with his daughter or what deal they had made.

"You know I'm marrying Yah-Yah soon, not to mention we have a son together." I stood up and got ready to walk out because this conversation is over.

"She is beneath you, and I would never allow you to marry her. I only accept your son because he's yours, although I'm not even sure about that these days."

"Don't ever disrespect my girl or my seed again. If anything, I'm beneath her. It was nice meeting y'all. I'll get up with you on the block, bro."

"If you refuse this offer then I have no choice but to cut ties with you. You're going against this family and everything we stand for. This is your last chance. It's either her or this family."

"Well, I guess this is goodbye. I choose my girl and my son."

I walked and bumped into my mother heading back out. She had tears in her eyes, which let me know that she knew about this shit the whole time. I'm almost positive she didn't speak up for her grandson on me. Her silence spoke volumes. I kissed her on the cheek and got the fuck out of dodge. I would give all this shit up and work a nine to five before I leave Yah-Yah. As I headed to the crib, I wondered if Yasir knew about that bullshit. Hell, the more I drove, the more I thought. How come Yasir couldn't marry her? They know Yah-Yah, and I have been building a life together, so it's beyond me why they would think I would be cool with that bullshit.

Chapter Three

YAH-YAH

It had only been twenty-four hours, and I was missing Yahmeen like crazy. I had called several times, but I knew he wasn't going to answer. I had pissed him clean off. When he gets like this, it's just best to let him cool off. At the same time, it had never got to a point where he physically took my ass to my parents' house. Just thinking about everything has me feeling bad about the way I go about shit. At the same time, it's like that's the only way I can get him to see how I feel.

"Ma, can you watch Jr. for me?"

"Where the hell you going? You know I only babysit on special occasions and when you have to take care of business." I rolled my eyes at my mother because she was being typical Boss Lady and had an attitude for no reason.

"I know, ma. I need to run and grab us some stuff from the mall. In case you forgot I don't have anything to wear. I promise I'm coming right back."

"That's not business, and I don't feel sorry about your ass not having any clothes. Keep clowning, and you won't have nothing."

I rolled my eyes at her and handed Jr to her. I hauled ass getting out of the door before she started back talking shit. I wasn't going to no damn mall. My ass was going to find my man. I love sleeping at my momma's house, but sleeping in bed with my nigga feels a lot better.

ૐ

It only took me about thirty minutes to make it home because there was no traffic. When I pulled up, Yahmeen was washing his favorite car. I think he loves that Porsche more than he loves me. I took notice of his facial expression. He looked like he was pissed at my presence, but I didn't care. I took a deep breath before stepping out of the car.

"We need to talk," I said as I approached him, but he ignored me. That alone made me mad, so I snatched the hose out of his hand.

"Don't do that, Yah-Yah! Today is not the day for your bullshit," he gritted as he snatched the hose from me. He turned his back to me, and I was trying my best not to spazz out. He knows I hate it when he does that shit.

"Really Meen? You still mad at me. I came over here to make shit right and you all in your feelings.

"Hell yeah, I'm still mad because you're not supposed to be here! In case you didn't get the picture, you live with your parents now. That's what you wanted, right?"

"No! That's not what I wanted. This is my house just as much as it is yours. I stayed out of it for one night, and I won't be staying out of it another night. I'm about to go get Jr., and then I'm coming home. I don't give a fuck what you say."

Before I knew it, he dropped the hose and rushed me so hard.

"Don't bring your ass back here until you learn to put some motherfucking respect on my name. I know you come from a family that doesn't mind getting their hands dirty! However, what you won't do is act like I'm some type of fuck nigga!

Take your ass back to your parents' house and don't come back until you put some motherfucking respect on my name. I'm Yahmeen Sr., not Jr.! Learn the difference, Ka'Jaiyah. Fuck on with this bullshit!"

He pushed me towards my car and kicked over the plants and garden statues that sat in our driveway. He walked inside the house and slammed the door without looking back at me.

For the first time in our relationship, he had me wanting to cry, but I refused to. He had me fucked up if he thought I was about to kiss his ass. I decided to go ahead and head to the mall to grab some shit. Instead of sitting around sulking, I was about to go out and enjoy myself. I've been sitting home being a damn mother while's he's been running the streets. I don't see why I can't run the motherfucking streets too.

ஃ

♫How would you like it
  If I do the things you do
  Put you on do not disturb
  And entertain this dude...♫

Queen Naija's song "Medicine" blasted through the speakers at Club Diamond. Heaven and I were kicking it in our private section. It felt so good to be out with my girl Heaven. It had been a minute since we had really been out and kicked it. Lil Dro be tripping hard on my girl. I swear he's begging for us to jump on his ass again. We were singing at the top of our lungs because we felt every word Queen Naija was saying. Lil Dro and Yahmeen had us so fucked up if they thought this shit was so sweet.

"It's time for me to go. Lil Dro and the rest of the crew just walked in, and I'm not in the mood for his shit."

"Girl, please! Dro better not come over here with that bullshit." No sooner than I spoke the words, here he comes walking his ass over to us.

"Where's my daughter at, Heaven?"

"Your momma came and got her this morning. Had you came home last night or called, you would know that."

I wanted to say something, but I know that I needed to mind my business. I had my own problems to deal with. I'm going to stay out of it, but he better not even think about hitting her.

"Let me holla at you real quick." I just knew Heaven was going to put up a fight, but she didn't.

"Please don't start your shit, Lil Dro."

"Chill, Yah-Yah, she's good. I just want to talk to her for a minute, that's all. Be easy, Killa." He smirked and walked off with Heaven in tow.

I sat back and continued to sip on my Patrón. I had to blink my eyes a couple of times to make sure I wasn't drunk. In the distance, I peeped Yahmeen, Yasir, and some Arab looking bitch walking into another section on the other side of the club. I knocked back the rest of my shot, and I took double steps getting my ass over to that section.

"Oh shit!" Yasir mumbled, but I heard his ass.

"What's going on, Yahmeen? Who the fuck is this?"

"Ain't shit going on, Yah-Yah? This is Raja. She's the daughter of one of my father's associates. They're in town, and he wanted us to show her around the Chi. Since we're asking questions, why aren't you at the crib with my son?" Yahmeen stared at me, and something was telling me that there was more to this hoe.

"He's with my parents where you dropped us off at in case you forgot. When you're done entertaining this hoe, I'll be home. When I say home, I mean the place where we live."

"We discussed this, and you know what it is. Don't start your shit, Ka'Jaiyah. You need to go to your parents' house and get our son. I'll call you tomorrow." He spoke so damn nonchalant, and that pissed me off. He had me fucked up trying to play me in front of this bitch. He's definitely going to regret that shit.

"Where were you at?" Heaven asked when I made it back over to our section.

"Talking to Yahmeen. Let's go. He got me so fucked up right now.

"What happened?" she asked as we headed out to the valet to get the car.

"That nigga over there entertaining some hoe that he claims is a family friend. He's talking all nonchalant to me like I won't tear this motherfucking club up!"

Heaven shook her head cause she knows it's hard as fuck to turn me down when I turn up. Yahmeen just played with me for the last time. Once valet came around with the car, I went well past the speed limit making it to my house. Getting out of the car, I headed in the back to the tool shed to get some gasoline. Going inside the house with the key, I started pouring gasoline all over the house.

"Please, Yah-Yah, don't do this shit! Yahmeen is going to kill you!" Heaven pleaded.

"Fuck Yahmeen!"

I continued to pour gasoline all over the house. All my life I've been Ka'Jaiyah, but tonight I'm Left Eye. I wasn't trying to hear shit! That nigga forgot who the fuck I am and trying to handle me in front of some bitch. If he doesn't want me to come home and insist that I stay at my parents' house, then he won't be able to have a house to come home to! That nigga wants to fight with me, well it's war. I lit the match, threw it, grabbed Heaven scary ass and got the fuck out of dodge!

"I can't believe you just set your own house on fire!" Heaven said in disbelief.

"Fuck that house! My daddy will buy me a new one." I flamed up my blunt and watched in the distance as the house burnt to the ground.

"I don't think you should have done that, Yah-Yah."

"What should I have done, Heaven? Let him handle me any kind of way. Nah! I'll leave that to you."

"What's that supposed to mean?"

"It means I'm not like you. I don't just let a nigga walk all over me and treat me like shit. You let Lil Dro mistreat the fuck out of you, and I'm sorry I can't let Yahmeen do me that way."

I hated to have to go in on Heaven, but that soft shit was starting to get on my nerves.

"I'm glad to know how you really feel, but let me enlighten you on some real shit. While Lil Dro really is taking me through it, Yahmeen treats your ass like a queen. Your ass doesn't see it though because you're so busy trying to prove a point to that man. If you think burning down your house will make him act right, you're sadly mistaken. This ain't did shit but show that man another side of you that he might not want to fuck with. Y'all supposed to be married in a couple of months and you walking around here like he some regular ass nigga you fuck with from time to time. You had better stop it Ka'Jaiyah before you lose that man for good. Take me to my car please."

I didn't have a come back I just wanted to get her to her car so that I can go get my baby. Just thinking about him, I realized I had burnt up all his shit. I wanted to cry, but I didn't want to do it in front of Heaven. I love my friend, but I didn't want to give her the satisfaction of knowing she right. Maybe later but not right now.

As I headed towards my parents' house, I knew I had fucked up. My ass chickened out quick and couldn't bring myself to go there. My phone was going off like crazy, and I knew they knew what the fuck I did. Word travels quickly when your father runs shit. I continued to drive around aimlessly not sure of what to do. My phone was still going off like crazy. Everybody was calling me. I only decided to go home when my Uncle Malik crazy start sending me threatening messages talking about he gone call DCFS on my ass. I swear he's so damn petty and childish. By the time I decided to head home, the sun was coming up. The driveway was damn near packed with cars. I quickly jumped out and headed inside to face the music. My momma was about to go crazy on my ass. Walking inside, everybody stopped talking and just stared at me.

"Damn, who died?" I laughed a little trying to lighten the mood. Of course, I failed miserably. No one was smiling or taking this shit lightly.

"Give me that extension cord! I'm about to beat your ass like your daddy should've. Do you have any idea what the hell is going on, Yah-Yah? Your ass could go to jail for this shit. If your ass is in jail that leaves Lil Bin Laden out here in the world by himself. Do you really want your child in DCFS custody?"

"No Uncle Malik, I don't, but I'm sure you'll be the one that calls in on me? I rolled my eyes at his ass for playing so much. He knows I hate when he calls my baby Lil Bin Laden.

"You damn right! I've stood around and watched you abuse these animals for years. I refuse to let you do my phew phew in. You thought it was a game when I texted your ass about calling DCFS!"

"Bye, Uncle Malik. Whatever happens, my baby is gone be good.

My parents got him, and I don't have anything to worry about. I did what I did, and I'm not sorry!" I stated matter of factly.

"You think this shit a game, Ka'Jaiyah Kenneth?" my mother asked as she started walking towards me. My Aunt Barbie grabbed her before she could make it over to me.

"I don't think it's a game. What am I supposed to do or say? I burned the house down and now what!" I'm trying to see why they so mad. It's not like they burned it down and had to deal with the consequences, so I'm lost.

"Why the fuck would you burn your own house down?" my father asked sternly.

"Don't ask me! Ask Yahmeen. His ass knows exactly why I did it." I saw my father move closer, but I didn't know he had smacked the fuck out of me until I hard the ringing in my ear.

"Really Daddy?" I cried. I was in shock and extremely hurt behind my father's actions. I don't even think my father has ever put his hands on me, so this definitely has me in my feelings.

"Let me tell me you something with your disrespectful ass! Make that the last time you pop slick to your mother or me. Over the years I've let your motherfucking mouth get way too slick. You've been walking around here like everybody owes you something— news flash this world doesn't owe you shit. You have to get out here and grind for whatever the fuck you want. That's what Yahmeen does day in and day out. While you're walking around bitching, crying, and nagging, that man is getting his shit out the mud. He's taking penitentiary and cemetery risks to take care of his family, but it ain't good enough for you. You're lucky that man doesn't beat your ass behind what the fuck you've done. Your ass has burnt your home to the ground trying to get some attention. Not once did you think about your motherfucking son! Everything you all own was in that house. How could you be so fucking stupid? You had no business over there anyway. He asked for his space, and you should have given him that.

"Daddyyy! You don't understand! We were at the club, and he was trying to front on me in front of some chick. He pissed me off telling me not to come to the house. If I can't live in the house he got for me, then he shouldn't be able to," I cried, trying my best to get some type of sympathy.

'"You can stop it with them crocodile ass tears! They don't work for me anymore. That is no excuse for burning down y'all house. You better hope he don't press charges on your crazy ass. Get the fuck out of my sight before I hit your ass again. I don't even want to look at your ass. I'm disappointed in you Ka'Jaiyah, and it's going to take a lot for me to deal with you going forward."

My daddy had tears in his eyes, and that hurt me. In all of my years on this earth, I have never seen my father in his feelings after disciplining us.

I cried as I went inside my old room where my baby slept. I felt like shit for making his life hard. We shouldn't be here we should be at our home. At the moment I needed to try and fix things with Yahmeen. Pulling out my cell phone I tried to call him over and over again, but it was going straight to voicemail. He had blocked me, and that had me hyperventilating. I had finally pushed him away for good.

Chapter Four

THUG

There isn't a word in the dictionary that can describe the love I have for my children. I would kill a brick and a building for all of them. Over the years, I've displayed some fucked up behavior in front of them, and I don't like that shit at all. My *I don't give a fuck* attitude has rubbed off on Yah-Yah, and it's all bad. I never thought I would have to smack some sense into one of my daughters. I'll fuck my sons up though cause their boys who have grown into men who tend to forget who run shit. At the same time, they don't give me hell like that damn Ka'Jaiyah. Her ass got me smoking Newport's again cause she stressing me the fuck out.

"You okay, babe?"

"No, I'm not okay. I just put my hands on my daughter." I had to wipe the tears that had fallen because I never thought in a million years that I would ever do that.

"Don't you even do that shit to yourself, babe! She's lucky all you did was slap the fuck outta her. I had every intention of beating her ass like a bitch in the streets. I knew sooner or later her behavior would get to you. Give me a kiss. I'm so proud of you for slapping her disrespectful ass." Tahari kissed and hugged me, but that shit didn't make me feel better.

"Let me go drop this money off to my people to sweep this shit under the rug and make it look like an accidental fire."

"But Yahmeen sent the video of her crazy ass dousing the house with gasoline."

"I know. He reached out and said he would never press charges against her. At the same time, he's done with her. He just wants to raise his son, and that's it. I can't be mad at him though. He's actually better than I am because I would've broken my foot off in her ass for that shit.

"I told her that man was going to get tired of her shit. It's too early, but I need a damn drink. This shit makes no sense at all. Go ahead. I'll cook breakfast so you can eat when you get back home. Don't let Ka'Jaiyah stress you out. This will make her grow the fuck up watch what I tell you. Broken hearts don't feel good. They make you boss up in the worse way. We can't help her with that. She has to figure it out on her own. She comes from a strong bloodline, so I know she got this. You handle that, and when you get back, I'm gone handle you." She winked her eye and walked off.

That's Boss Lady for you. She's always trying to figure out a way to make a nigga feel good.

"Come on, bro. Let's ride."

"I know your ass wasn't crying, nigga! I'll beat London, Zaria, and Barbie's ass and won't blink too many times," Malik said as we hopped inside of the car. I just laughed at his dumb ass.

"Bro, that shit got me so fucked up!"

"I know it does. Yah-Yah is nutty as hell. We just have to get her the help she needs. Y'all think I just be joking. That girl ain't right in the head. She's been a couple of bricks short of a building all her life."

"She got too much of me in her. That girl is gone be a beast if she realizes what the fuck is in within her. Yah-Yah has the ability to be the next Griselda Blanco. She don't give a fuck bro, and that's what scares me about her.

"I've been scared of her because I been saw it. She is gone be good though. Let's handle this shit. I have to go to marriage counseling later with Barbie." He flamed up a blunt and passed it to me.

"She got your ass sitting with a shrink, huh?"

"If I want to keep getting pussy I have to go. Shit, I'll have all the fucking counseling she wants if it means I can keep fucking. Since I'm faithful now and can't have no side bitches, I be trying to knock a lining out her ass. I teach her ass about trying to be selfish with the dick."

"Your ass is hell, bro." I shook my head at this silly nigga. He keeps cracking on Yah-Yah like his ass is not nutty as fuck right along with her. That's why they stay at each other throat.

Just thinking about her and her actions made me feel fucked up all over again. I needed Yah-Yah to get her shit together. I don't want her to be the fuck up of the family. She's a good mother. I see the way she takes care of her son. As hard as she is with animals, she loves that little boy. This shit has got to show her that its time to grow the fuck up before it's too late. That would kill me as a father to see her lose everything and not be able to get it back. At the same time, I have to sit this one out and allow her to find her place in this world.

Chapter Five

YAHMEEN

It was taking everything inside of me not to kill Yah-Yah's ass. My son was the main reason why I couldn't. I admit I could have handled her better in front of Raja, but that attitude of hers pissed me off. Had I known she would go off the deep end and burn our fucking house down, I would have just told her crazy ass to go home. Yah-Yah's thinking I just didn't want her back home with me. I was simply trying to teach her ass a lesson that ended up backfiring on me.

"I told you that girl was crazy as hell. Look at this shit!" Yasir said, looking around at all the rubble that was once our home.

I shook my head looking at what was left of our son's baby book—all of his first memories gone down the drain because his mother had to prove a point. I bent down and picked up what was left of it. I was speechless looking at the carnage around me. This shit left a bad taste in my mouth in regards to her. I really needed my space from her. All I want to do is take care of my son. Hell, she'll be taken care of too, but my mind is not in the right place to deal with her shit.

"Really? This is the woman you want me to accept as your wife?"

"Not right now. The last thing I need to hear is this."

I walked away from my father and talked with the fire marshal. After speaking with her pops, I found out he got shit squared away. I was pissed at Yah-Yah, but I never want to see her behind bars. That would be a fuck nigga move.

❧

It had been a week since the fire, and I had yet to speak to Yah-Yah or see my son. A nigga really needed to calm down before seeing her in person. I had so much rage inside of me that I might fuck around and kill her ass then be in a war with her people. Since she couldn't get in contact with me, she had been blowing my brother and parents' phones up. Regardless of anything I did, I owe her the right to know we were done to her face. It would only be so long before we would end up bumping heads in the streets. I've witnessed her act an ass enough in public.

Besides dealing with Yah-Yah, I had been dealing with so much backlash from my parents. Of course, my father was through the roof behind her burning the house down. That gave him more ammunition to push for me to be with Raja. He even went so far as to have her father leave her here in the states. I have a badass feeling about that right there. I'm not surprised by my father's actions. I am however mad at my mother for even suggesting that we get custody of my son. She had me fucked up because I would never take my son away from Yah-Yah. She might be crazy, but she's a wonderful mother. I could never take Jr. away from her.

Without calling, I popped up at her parents' house. Since we weren't speaking at the moment, I felt more comfortable catching her nutty ass off guard.

"What's good, Yahmeen?" Kaine greeted me as I walked inside the house.

"Hey, bro." We dapped it up, and I then did the same with KJ and Kash.

Despite all of the beef I used to have with Kaine and Kash, we've all become quite cordial. They have their thing going on in the street, and I have mine. We make sure to steer clear of each other's blocks. That's how shit has been peaceful. The last thing I need is a drug war. A nigga got enough shit going on.

"You came over here just in time. We're getting ready to have a gathering for Grandma Peaches. She's a year cancer free, and we're about to have the party of the year. You should stay, bro. I'm sure Ka'Jaiyah would like that," KJ offered as he handed me a blunt. I took a couple of pulls and handed it back.

"As much as I would love to stay and celebrate with Ms. Peaches, I can't. I've actually come to talk to Yah-Yah. Where's she at?"

"She went to the store with my OG. It's a good thing you're here. We were just about to have a meeting with my pops. Why don't you sit in with us?"

"Nah I'm good. That's some business between you all."

The way KJ was looking at me while he sipped his Rémy looked suspect as hell. That added with inviting me to a meeting I have nothing to do with. Yeah, I'm good on all of that.

"Actually, I was going to be discussing you anyway. It's a good thing you showed up." This nigga KJ was tripping.

Looking over at Kaine and Kash, they were smirking. At that moment, I was regretting leaving my damn gun in the car. These niggas were no jokes out here in these streets, so I know their ass on one with a nigga. I hope they didn't think I was bitch nigga or something. KJ walked off, and I followed him back to what looked like a conference room. Thug and Malik were already sitting in there.

"How nice of you to join us, Yahmeen? When KJ propositioned that we bring you on the team, I was skeptical. Seeing that you're here that means you agreed," Thug spoke as he puffed on a Cuban cigar.

"Actually, pops, I hadn't propositioned him yet. He just has good timing."

"Y'all hungry?" Ms. Tahari spoke as she walked inside the room.

"Really Boss Lady! You know not to come in here when the door is closed."

"And you know I still walk in. Hey Yahmeen, I'm glad you're here. When you get finished in here, I would like to have a word with you. Hurry the hell up before the food gets cold. Today is about family. You motherfuckers refuse to put that street shit on the shelf for a day." She slammed the door hard as hell, and it made me laugh a little.

"Don't laugh at my pain lil nigga because then I would have to laugh at yours. Yah-Yah is far worse than her mother!"

"Ms. Ceclie, you has my sympathy!" Malik said, patting me on the shoulder. I couldn't help but laugh because this nigga was funny as fuck.

"Yah-Yah is not at that bad!"

"That's my sister, and I love her dearly. However, I wouldn't wish her on any man in this world. I grew up with her and knew she was a pyromaniac. Sleep with one eye open, my nigga!" Kash spoke up and handed me a blunt to flame up.

"Enough about Yah-Yah. Let's talk about this proposition," I spoke up as put on my game face on.

"Well, we were thinking you should join our camp. Your name is ringing out here in the streets. Plus, anyone who marries into this family is usually a part of the team anyway. Consider this your initiation," KJ spoke like a true leader, and I could tell Thug was proud of him.

That shit had me feeling some type of way in regards to my father. He was never proud, and nothing was ever good enough. Everyone else in the room was staring at me and waiting for my response.

"That's an honor to be invited into your family. However, I have my own family business to run, not to mention I have some pertinent issues that I need to discuss with my father and brother before making such a hasty decision. I mean no disrespect, but I have to decline."

"No disrespect taken. Actually, Yahmeen I was hoping you said that. It shows you're loyal to your blood. The offer will always be on the table. Kaine, show him out. I'm sure he would love to see his son." Thug saluted me, and I gave him a head nod before Kaine walked me out.

As I headed outside to talk to Yah-Yah, I silently prayed that I had done the right thing choosing my family. Lately, they had all been moving shady, including Yasir. While they're plotting on me, I'm ten steps ahead of them. At the same time, I pray I don't have to do what I have in mind. The backyard was filled with their family, and of course, all eyes were on me.

"Boy, you is one fine Puerto Rican!" Aunt Gail said as she winked her eye at me.

"Actually, I'm from the Middle East, but thank you, beautiful."

"Oh shit, niece! That nigga is checking for your auntie.

"That damn boy don't want your old shriveled up pussy ass," Aunt Sherita said as she marinated the ribs with some sauce that I could have sworn smelled like Patrón.

"Don't worry about it, bitch. I know somebody like it. Ain't that right, Mike baby?"

"You got that right, Fat Cat!" he yelled as he flipped some chicken on the grill.

I couldn't do shit but laugh. Every time I come around, it's nothing but laughs and love. This family is bat shit crazy. I'm lost as to why they're so confused about Yah-Yah's mental state.

"We need to talk, Ka'Jaiyah. Come outside to the car."

"Oh, now you want to talk to me! Bye Yahmeen. Here spend some time with your son." She basically pushed him into my arms and walked away. I tried not to notice, but her mother was shaking her head as Yah-Yah passed her on the way into the house.

"Hey, daddy's man." I kissed him on the forehead and walked inside the house to find Yah-Yah. She was sitting in the living room on her phone. She was trying her best to ignore me, so I snatched the phone from her hand.

"Give me my phone back!"

"Hell nah! Calm your ass down. I have some shit I need to say, and I need your undivided attention."

"Make it quick. I'm hungry." I held my composure and decided not to feed into her pettiness.

"Cut the bullshit, Yah-Yah! You're sitting here like you didn't burn our house to the ground! While you were pouring that gasoline all over the house, did you ever take a minute and think about him? As a parent that made you selfish!"

"You're the one that's selfish, Yahmeen. How could you just put me out of the house like it wasn't mine too? Not to mention you went in on me in front of your bitch!"

For the first time, I saw tears in her eyes, and I was glad. That showed she had feelings because her behavior shows the opposite.

"You were the one who acted like our home was the last place you wanted to be. That added with you constantly doing disrespectful shit like I'm not the man of the house. We were about to get married. Instead of you acting like a fiancée, you were acting like a side bitch that didn't know her place. As far as that bitch goes, she was a business associate. You would have known that had you not come into the section acting a fool."

"Whatever Yahmeen! Are you done?"

"Actually, I'm finished. This right here is not working for me. You need to be single because being in a relationship is not your thing. This is how this is going to go. Every month I'll give you twenty thousand. Here's the first payment. By the end of the week, you'll have a new home that will be fully furnished. All you have to do is get clothes for you and Jr. Here is a black card. I have a limit on it, so don't think you'll be out splurging. It's for emergencies only, Ka'Jaiyah. I'll get Jr. every other weekend and whatever day you want during the week. All I ask is that you give me some notice. I'm going to take him right now. I'll call you later."

"It's that easy, huh. You love me one minute, and the next you're done with me?"

She quickly wiped the tears from her face, but it meant nothing to me. She needed to feel this shit so that in the future, she knows how to handle me. I have every intention of coming back for her, but she needs to get her shit together first.

"This shit is not easy at all. It's actually the hardest thing I've ever had to do. It's embarrassing to be out here in these streets letting motherfuckers know how I feel about you and you out here showing you don't give a fuck about me. So, yeah Yah-Yah just like that I'm done. I love the fuck out of you, but I can't do this shit with you anymore. I'll check on you later." I kissed her on the jaw and left with my son in tow.

It hurt me to hurt her, but she had left me no choice. This was actually a good move on my end. It would help with the plan that I was cooking. Lord knows I didn't need her fucking shit up with her craziness.

Chapter Six

HEAVEN

I had been kicking my own ass for not going on an extended vacation with my family. That's what I get for not following my first mind. The main reason why I stayed back was because Lil Dro was acting a fool behind me taking our daughter. My stupid ass stayed back, and the nigga comes home whenever the fuck he feels like it. I'm literally over this bullshit with him. I love him, but I've grown extremely tired and irritated with his behavior. Our daughter is now two years old and bad as ever.

Some days I wish I had waited to have a baby because life would be different. Now, don't get me wrong I love Reminisce. It's just that Dro wasn't ready for a baby. He takes care of us financially, but he is so disconnected from us, and it hurts. Lately, his behavior has been so off the wall that I don't know what the day will bring. That's not even the bad part. The nigga has a whole bitch out here and thinks I'm going to keep accepting this shit.

Lil Dro has done a complete three sixty, and I have no idea who the hell he is these days. The way I'm feeling I really need to vent, but I can't since my human diary was losing her fucking mind. I'm still in shock behind Yah-Yah burning the house to the ground. Then she has the nerve to be mad at me for voicing my opinion. She might as I well stay mad. I said what I said, and I meant it. Her ass is walking around with a nigga that loves her, and she simply can't appreciate it. I really hope and pray they fix things because they were made for each other.

The sound of the garage door opening excited me. It had been two days since Lil Dro had come home. I was so happy our daughter was sleeping. He and I indeed needed to have a conversation.

Making my way down the stairs, I noticed he was putting money in the wall safe.

"Are you hungry?" I asked as I approached him.

"Nah! I ate already." He was obviously in a mood, and it irritated me. The nigga had a lot of nerve to be walking around this bitch with an attitude after being gone for two days.

"What did you eat?"

"Food. What's with all the questions?"

"I can't ask you questions, Khiandre?" I stepped closer to him, and he was looking everywhere but at me.

"Don't start with me, Heaven. I swear to God I'll walk back out this bitch and it will be a week before you see me again," he spoke through gritted teeth as he basically pressed his forehead against mine with force. Had he done it any harder, he would have headbutted the shit out of me.

"That's what you want to do anyway. Go ahead to that bitch. I don't even care anymore. Fuck you and that bitch." I muffed his ass, and without hesitation, he slapped the fuck out of me. Tears immediately fell as the taste of blood filled my mouth.

"How many motherfucking times have I told you about putting your hands on me? Don't stand there with a shocked ass look on your face. I've been telling you this shit for the longest. Stop questioning me about what I do. You know all about Shieka, so stop with the fucking foolery. Next time you put your hands on me, I'm going to beat your ass." He pushed me out of the way, and he walked out of the back door."

For what seemed like an eternity I stood in the same place crying my ass off. His anger had been escalating lately. This was a first for him to put his hands on me. My father would kill his ass if he knew what was going on. No one really knows what's going on, but I need to at least reach out to Khia so that she can talk to him about his behavior. I'm officially fed up with his bullshit, and I can't take it anymore. I've stayed this long for the sake of our daughter, and at this point, I'm not sure that's enough anymore.

⚜

True to his word, it had been a week, and I hadn't heard from him. I was no longer sad about the situation. I was pissed. Lil Dro could do whatever he wanted to do to me, but what he wasn't going to do is play with our daughter. How could he not want to at least call and check on her? I've never been the confrontational type, but this nigga makes me want to fight him.

He had been fucking with the bitch Shieka for so long that I knew where the bitch worked, lived, and hung at. I just never wanted to be that type of chick that blames a woman behind a nigga. However, she fucks with him and knows he slacks with his daughter. That alone makes me have beef with the bitch, not to mention I just been looking for a reason to fight her. The bitch be all over social media with her sneak dissing, and I've been ignoring the shit. This morning I woke up on bullshit simply because Lil Dro thinks he can keep fucking with me. Ever since I've given birth to my daughter, he's been so wishy-washy with me. One minute he wants a damn family, and the next minute being a family man is too much.

Granted he's young, but that's no excuse. I'm young as well, but my daughter is everything to me. I'm the one who was pregnant and didn't know until I gave birth. The moment I looked at her, I knew I had to grow up. It was about time Lil Dro did the same. He wants to live a double life and slack in his daddy duties. The nigga has left me no choice but to act a fool with his ass. Apparently, he was at his bitch's house laid up. I know because she posts everything they do. Before heading over to her house, I dropped my daughter off to my grandma. I had to lie about where I was going. The last thing I need is Sherita on a mission like this. She would for sure cut up behind me.

⚜

About an hour later, I was sitting on the hood of Lil Dro's car waiting for him to come out the hoe's house. I wasn't knocking on that bitch door or stepping foot on her property. I wasn't trying to go to jail for trespassing. I flamed up a blunt and puffed on it until he came outside. I knew he knew I was outside because I saw the curtains moving. The front door opened, and I jumped off the hood of the car. She came outside and leaned up against the porch frame. My heart sank as she rubbed her protruding belly. This bitch was pregnant. That was something she never let be known on her social media.

"Why the fuck you come out here? Didn't I tell your ass to stay in the house?" This nigga was yelling while he put his shirt over his head.

"I'm tired of this shit, Dro. You're playing with her and me. I can't keep doing this. My baby has to be swept under the rug, and he is no secret. You need to tell her we're together now."

My eyes bulged out of my head hearing her say that. He was speechless. I could tell he didn't want her to say that part, but I'm glad she did. The shit gave me clarity, and it's what I needed to move forward with my life. I'm young and beautiful with the rest of my life ahead of me. The last thing I need is to waste my life on a nigga that clearly doesn't want me.

"He doesn't have to tell me anything. It's obvious y'all together. All I ask is that you take care of the daughter you have. The only reason I came over here was to confront you about spending time with her. Feel free to call whenever you get the chance. I'll be moved out of the house by the end of the week." I tried to walk back towards my car, but he quickly made his way over to me and pulled me back.

"Where the fuck you think you going? Your ass just pops up over on bullshit and try to leave."

"Let me go, Khiandre! I'm over your bullshit. You want to act stupid with me while you're over here building a new family. What the fuck did I do to you? What about Remy Ma and me? You said fuck us, and I don't know why! Please tell me why! I deserve that much, Khiandre. Do you even really love me or our daughter?"

At that moment, I was crying my eyes out. I didn't care that Shieka was right there witnessing it. My momma would kill me if she knew I was out in the streets showing my emotions, but I couldn't help it. I'm so hurt right now that I couldn't even hold the tears in if I wanted to.

"Don't ever question my love for either of you. I'm sorry about this situation. I was going to tell you when the time was right!"

"When was that going to be? After she gave birth. Nigga, fuck you! You a lame ass nigga, and I wish I never knew your dog ass. My daughter doesn't need your ass for shit, so stay the fuck away from us you bitch ass nigga!" I kept muffing his ass as I spoke. He was getting angrier and angrier. He wanted to hit me so bad.

"Is there a problem here?" a police officer asked from the driver seat of a squad car that pulled up in front of us.

"Nah! Everything is good, officer," I said and walked away from his ass.

Pulling away from the curb, I tried my best not to cry, but the tears flowed. This nigga had played me in the worst way. Here I am thinking he just wanted his cake and eat it too, and all along he was building a new family. My ass was so distracted that I ran a red light and a car smacked me so hard that I went airborne. It was the last thing I remembered before blacking out.

"Thank God, you're okay!" my mother said as she kissed my forehead.

After being in a coma for two days, I had finally woken up. The accident was serious, and they said I was lucky to be alive. All I keep seeing is a car hitting me. The shit is traumatizing as hell. I don't think I ever want to get behind the wheel again. I'm blessed to be here because the last thing I ever want to do is leave my daughter alone. Lord, knows her father wouldn't do his part.

"I'm okay, ma. Stop crying." She had been crying like crazy since I woke up.

"I know. I was so scared getting that phone call. Your dad and I caught the first flight out straight to you. The whole family has been here, including the boy who pulled you from the wreck.

"What boy?"

"Yahmeen's brother Yasir is the person you were in an accident with. He pulled you from the wreck and drove you to the hospital himself. He's been here ever since."

Just hearing that Yasir was the one who rescued me had me thinking about how much he used to like me. I just could never give him the time of day because I was in love with Dro's stupid ass, not to mention Dro was always trying to be on bullshit with Yasir.

"Is Dro here?"

"Of course, he's here. Why wouldn't he be, Heaven?"

My mother truly had no idea about his ass. Lil Dro had done such a good job at putting on a façade for everyone. I would just keep it to myself about us no longer being together. In due time they will find out about the shit he's been up to. That's the main thing I'm afraid of because my pops don't fucking play about me. Once you fuck me over, then here he comes, and I can't control that crazy motherfucker. At the same time, I don't even want drama within our families. All the bullshit has died down, and I want to keep it that way. Before I could ask my mother any more questions, there was a knock at the door.

"Come in!" she yelled. My heart fluttered as someone walked in with a huge bouquet of roses along with a beautiful, red teddy bear. I couldn't see their face at first but soon learned it was Yasir. He was still fine as fuck even with a patch on his forehead.

"These are for you. I'm happy you're okay."

"You didn't have to do this. Thank you for rescuing me."

"No problem. How are you feeling?" He pulled up a chair, and I took notice of my mom with this weird smirk on her face.

"Like I was in a car accident." I managed to laugh a little, and it hurt like hell since I had some broken ribs and a collapsed lung.

"Right." He smiled and was getting ready to say something but in walked Dro. His presence alone put a damn damper on my spirits. He had a mean ass scowl on his face, and I was sure he was about to start some shit.

"Heaven was just looking for you, Khiandre," my momma spoke up and lied. She knows damn well I wasn't actually looking for him.

"I just wanted to check on you and make sure that you're okay." Yasir stood to leave, and honestly, I didn't want him too.

"Thanks, Yasir." He winked at me and walked out of the door. I was happy my mother left too. That crazy smirk on her face was starting to bother me.

"I'm glad to see you woke. You had me scared for a minute." He came over and kissed me on the forehead. I wondered did he think I couldn't remember the events that led up to my damn accident.

"Really? Does your baby momma know you were scared?"

"Don't do that, Heaven. Right now is not the time to discuss the shit that's going on with Shieka. The only thing that matters is that you're okay."

"You're so full of shit, Khiandre. Let me make this shit clear since you can't keep it real with me. We're done. I no longer expect anything from you outside of taking care of our daughter. Seeing how you move lately lets me know we're done. I just wish you had told me instead of stringing me along. I can forgive a lot of things, but not a baby. I can't keep sitting around waiting for you to love me. I've been doing that shit since Remy Ma was born, and I'm over it. Thank you for being here, but you can leave now."

He was the last person I wanted around me. Lil Dro was here putting on a façade for my family, and I wasn't here for it. This accident has me looking at life extremely different. All my life I've looked around at the women in my family going through shit with niggas, and I don't want to be that person. The first time a nigga cross me, he lost me. That's exactly the situation right here. I'm good on a relationship with Lil Dro.

"You really think you have a say so on when we're done? Newsflash Heaven, you don't. You're the mother of my daughter, and I refuse to let any nigga have you. You belong to me, and any nigga that thinks he can have you is going to feel me. We can do this the easy way or the hard way. The choice is yours."

"Leave, Lil Dro. Your ass got a whole bitch out here pregnant by you, and I'm supposed to just accept that. I'm sorry but the days of you feeling like you can handle me any kind of way is over. I'm gone be with who I want and when I want."

I turned my back to his crazy ass. He had me fucked up if he thought he could ever back me into a corner. I had lost all interest the moment I learned that bitch was carrying his baby. He needed to just focus on doing right by his daughter.

"Well, just keep your all black ready. Get some rest. I'll slide back through tomorrow."

He walked out of the room, and all I could do was think about his strange ass behavior. It was one thing for Lil Dro to be out with another woman, but it was something totally different to be talking about killing folks. Granted he is a part of Thug Legacy, and they play no games. At the same time, lately, his behavior has been off like he's bipolar or something. I never know which side of him I'm dealing with. No matter the case, I'm done with his crazy ass.

§♠

It had been a week since I had come home from the hospital, and I was over it. I was on strict bed rest, and I was going crazy. I wish I could be in the comfort of my own home, but my parents weren't having it. I swear I don't know where I would be without them, especially my daddy. He's been taking care of me around the clock, not to mention making sure my baby been good.

All week my mother had been talking shit because Dro hadn't come around or called for that matter. She and Khia had even exchanged words. Lil Dro is so damn stupid. He knows this shit will cause drama. Instead of him just doing his part, he would rather create issues. At this point, I'm no longer hiding his fucking secrets to save face.

Besides the issues with Lil Dro, I was in my feelings behind Yah-Yah not reaching out. Not only were we cousins, but she was my best friend. The fact that she had never reached out to check on me had me feeling some type of way. I understand that she was going through her shit with Yahmeen, but she could have at least called. If the shoe were on the other foot, I wouldn't hesitate to put everything to the side for her. I'm not surprised though. She has always been selfish as hell.

"Is everything okay with you and Lil Dro? Don't lie to me," my father spoke sternly. That let me know that he already knew something, so there was no need for me to try and lie.

"We aren't together anymore, daddy. I really don't even want to talk about it."

"Well, that's too bad because the shit I'm hearing about that lil nigga got me heated. Don't hold shit back. What the hell is up, Heaven?"

"He has a baby on the way with another girl."

"What the fuck you say?" my mother said as she walked all the way in the room.

"He has a baby on the way with another girl. Please promise me you all won't go acting crazy. I'm okay."

"That lil nigga is gone have to see me! I distinctly told that mother-fucker not to play games with you." My daddy was so mad that he knocked over the lamp.

"His momma is gone have to see me too. I now know why her ass been standoffish lately!"

"Please don't confront either of them! I was just in a bad car acci-dent that almost killed me. Lil Dro is not worth it. He's the last person I'm thinking about. This one time, please don't go shooting and killing up folks. Listen to me! I'm not a little girl anymore. I'm a grown woman with a child of my own. I know that y'all love me and don't play about me. At the same time, this is just one of those issues that I have to deal with on my own. I love how y'all love me, but this one time, I just need you all to let me stand on my own."

I could tell they were both mad, but I didn't care. One of the biggest problems in my relationship with Lil Dro was my parents. He hated that I was my daddy's daughter, and he was coming no matter what. Honestly, my parents had been a big part of my relationship. This time around, I just want to handle things my way. My father punched a hole on the wall and walked off. I knew he wouldn't take what I said lightly.

"You're right, Heaven. I'll let you handle this shit on your own. At the same time, he better do right by my grandbaby, or it's gone be some shit. You better treat him like shit too and don't let up. Go out and get you some good ass dick to make that nigga sick. I'll handle your daddy. You know he don't play about you, so Lil Dro definitely needs to get on his shit. I love you, Heaven. Now get you some rest.

Your dad and I have to head out to handle some business. Please follow the doctor's orders. I'm going to be calling Ginger to make sure." My mother kissed me on the forehead and left me alone.

My notification went off on my phone, and it was a text from Yasir. A smile instantly spread across my face. Since the accident, he checked on me all day every day, not to mention he sends flowers and candy every day. I swear he be having me blushing every time the things get delivered. I wasn't really sure what Yasir was doing, but I liked it. Right now I'm vulnerable, so that's most likely why I've become so smitten with him. Every time I tell myself he's just being nice because of the accident, he does something that shows he's genuine. Either way, he's giving me the attention I've been craving.

A knock at the door jarred me from my thoughts of Yasir. I kind of got excited because I was hoping it was my daily delivery from. That quickly subsided when I realized it was Lil Dro. He picked the wrong damn time to show up. My parents weren't feeling his ass at the moment.

"Hey, Heaven. I came to check on you and pick up Remy Ma."

"I'm good. I have no issue with you getting her, but it's been a week Dro. Why are you just now coming to see her? You haven't called or anything. What the fuck is up with that?"

"I'm sorry Heaven, but I have some shit going on right now. Can you please get her ready?"

This nigga must be on drugs or something. He refuses to acknowledge the fact that he has another damn baby on the way. He's literally walking around like nothing has transpired. That alone irritates me, but I wasn't about to give him the satisfaction of thinking I give a fuck. I have to be just as nonchalant as he's being about the situation.

"Ginger, can you please get the baby ready? You can pack her some overnight things as well."

"Yes, ma'am."

"Look I know this shit fucked up on my part, and I'm sorry. I can't change the fact that I made a fucked up decision, and it hurt you. One thing for sure and two for certain, I love you and my daughter more than anything in this world. Just know that everything is happening for a reason. You might not get it now, but in due time it will."

This nigga was so full of shit. I'm officially over his real stupid goofy ass.

"Yeah, I hear you, Khiandre! Just don't have my baby around that bitch or it's definitely going to be some shit."

"I would never take Remy Ma around no bitch. We'll be at my OG crib all weekend. Thanks for letting me get her."

"Let's make some shit real clear. I'm not doing this shit for you. I'm doing it for her. As much as I hate what you've done to me, I will never punish her. She loves you, and that's why I've been so angry with you about not spending time like you should. I'm hurt behind your actions because it's like you woke up one day and said fuck me. I refuse to ask what I did because I've done nothing."

Although I wasn't supposed to be up on my feet, I slowly got up and left his ass alone in the living room. I had nothing else to say to him. He just needed to do what he had to do for our daughter. That's it, and that's all.

Chapter Seven

YAH-YAH

As I looked around the new home Yahmeen had gotten me, I couldn't help but love it. The entire house was furnished from top to bottom. Both my baby and I had closets full of shit that was filled to the brim. Standing inside of my bedroom let me know that our break up was real. There weren't any remnants of Yahmeen. I was hoping that he was just teaching me a lesson, but this shit was beyond a lesson. We hadn't really had a decent conversation since he broke up with me. He would FaceTime our son, and that was it. The nigga had no words for my ass, and that was cool. I may be a lot of things, but one thing I'll never be is a bitch that begs a nigga to fuck with her. If he wanted out of the relationship then so be it. I'm not in the business of trying to keep a nigga that don't want to be kept.

This time apart from Yahmeen will probably do me good. I'm tired of being in that nigga's shadow. Everyone around me is expecting me to lose myself because I'm with a man like Yahmeen. I love him, but I want my own identity outside of him and who he is. I want to be known as Yah-Yah the baddest bitch, not the wife of Yahmeen. That might sound stupid, but I don't care. The last thing I want to do is become that nigga's shadow.

Besides dealing with Yahmeen and his shit, I had been thinking about Heaven. My selfishness had allowed me to not even check on her after her accident. I feel so fucked up about that it's hard for me to face her. My Aunt Sherita's birthday party is tonight, and I know she's going to be there. I really pray that she can forgive me because I need her more now than ever. Out of everybody in the world, she should be the last person I ever hurt. No matter what bullshit I do, she's always right there holding me down. I owe her an apology. I pray that she can accept it, and we go back to being best friends.

Since my son was with Yahmeen for the weekend, I decided to take me a much-needed nap. As I drifted off to sleep, all I could think about was where was I going from here. I need to find me some shit to do because I will not be spending my days in this house being a fucking old lady in the shoe. I'm too young for that shit. Plus, I'm single and ready to mingle. I need to get out here in these streets and get me a nigga to fuck with. I don't see why I can't. I'm positive Yahmeen is fucking bitches left and right. He just bet not let me catch it or see it. I'm beating bitches ass behind him. I don't care if we are broken up. We're together even when we not together. He just hasn't realized it yet.

❧

Walking into my Aunt Sherita's backyard, the party was in full swing. Of course, she was in the middle of the dance floor doing her thing. Aunt Gail was right with her. I swear they were like two peas in a pod. Of course, Grandma Peaches was off to the side embarrassed as hell. Gail and Sherita don't give a fuck about anything.

"It's about time you made it. I thought I was going to have to drag your depressed ass over here. Heaven is inside the house. Go and check on her." Aunt Sherita was twerking and talking to me at the same time. Uncle Dino didn't make it no better dancing behind her.

I was glad my parents hadn't arrived yet. It had been so hard being in the presence of my father, and he wouldn't even speak to me. If I walked inside of a room, he would walk out. My hurt ached each and every time. I was more than happy when Yahmeen had finally got the house ready for me to move in. I was going to lose my mind if I had to spend one more day in that house being ignored. My ass was more depressed behind my father being mad at me than Yahmeen. I know people don't understand, but the love I have for my father is beyond anything I can explain. My mother, on the other hand, only made sure I was straight during the time that I was there. She was still mad at me, but she also felt sorry for my ass. I could see it in her eyes, but Boss Lady was too stubborn to admit. I know she was low key happy my daddy was showing me tough love. My brothers and sisters were too. Kaine and Kash's retarded asses thought the shit was one big joke.

When I made it inside the house, I was surprised to see Yasir sitting on the couch with Heaven. I could tell she was irritated by my presence by the way that she rolled her eyes.

"What's good, sis?" Yasir asked as he got up and gave me a hug. I low key have always believed he didn't really care for me but tolerated me for the sake of his brother. It was always things that he did on the slick that Yahmeen didn't catch.

"Hey. What are you doing here?"

"I just came to check on Heaven and bring Ms. Sherita her birthday gift. I'm about to head out now. I'll check with you later, Heaven." He walked out of the back door, and that left Heaven and me alone. She was looking straight ahead refusing to even look at me.

"I know you're mad at me, and I'm sorry for not being here for you."

"I'm not mad at you, Yah-Yah. I'm disappointed in you. Had you been in an accident, I would have been right there beside you with bells on. I've always known your ass was selfish, but not selfish like this. At the same time, I'm happy you love me enough to apologize for your absence. After all, the Yah-Yah I know never apologizes."

We both laughed, and I walked over to the couch and wrapped my arms around her neck.

"How are you?"

"I'm doing good now. My ribs and lungs are healing really good. Hopefully, I can get out here in about another week or so. I'm tired of being on bed rest."

"Well, I'm happy that you're okay. I'm truly sorry for not being here for you. I have so much going on in my life that it's crazy."

"I heard. How are you doing now that you and Yahmeen are officially done?"

"I really don't know how to feel. I'm trying to deal with the fact that I'm living in this house and he doesn't. That added with the fact I think he's dealing with that bitch I saw him at the club with that night. I have to just accept the fact that he wants it to be over. At the same time, he needs to know that we're together even we not together. I'll play this role with Yahmeen if that's what he wants, but I'm not allowing him to be with another bitch. That's enough talk about me. What the hell is Yasir doing over here?" Heaven shook her head and laughed. I was dead ass serious though. If I can't have him no one can.

"Yasir's car is the car that I ended up hitting when I ran the red light that day. He's the one who got me to the hospital and everything. Yasir has been here with me every day, and I think that's what's helping me heal so fast. Every day he sends me a bouquet of roses and edible arrangements." Heaven's eyes sparkled as she spoke about Yasir. I hadn't seen such a glow in her eyes since she had Remy Ma.

"Where the hell is Lil Dro at while all of this is going on?"

"He's probably somewhere laid up with his baby momma, Shieka. That bitch is about to have his baby. That's how I ended up in the damn accident in the first place. I had become so fed up with his bullshit that I went to that bitch's house for his ass. This hoe came out of the house big ass hell. Lil Dro stepped out behind her looking like a deer in headlights. The whole scene let me know it was time for me to let that nigga go. After arguing with his stupid looking ass, I jumped in my car to get away from his ass. As I drove, so many emotions came over me that I wasn't paying attention to the road. My ass ended up running a red light slamming into Yasir. Shit has been crazy, but I'm happy to be alive and content with the fact that I'm no longer with his ass."

I sat speechless listening to Heaven. She was so calm as she spoke. My ass was not there yet. I would be beating Dro and that bitch's ass pregnant and all. I swear I wanted to go and find they ass myself, but I know I needed to chill out.

"I guess we've both been going through it. Hurry up and get well. We have some partying to do."

I kicked my feet up on the table and laid my head on her shoulder. It felt so good to be back on good terms with my best friend. Lord knows she's the only one who understands me.

"I'm about to kill this lil bitch! She done knocked my damn grill over coming to my house with this bullshit!" Aunt Sherita said as she came into the house.

"Who, grandma?"

"Some damn girl out here trying to fight Milania. Talking about she looking for Kaine."

I just shook my head because I knew the shit he was on was about to backfire on his ass. However, one thing side bitches are not allowed to do is pull up around family like it was sweet. I quickly got up and rushed outside to see everybody holding Milania back.

"Why the fuck are you here, Kionni?" Kaine asked like his stupid ass didn't know.

"I'm here because you not about to keep playing with me."

"Go your ass home Kionni before I let my dawg loose!"

As soon as he said that, I knew what time it was. I pulled my hair up into a high ponytail and got ready to kick her ass. Anytime Kaine said them words he wanted me to beat a bitch's ass for him.

"I'm not going no motherfucking where!"

As soon as the words left her mouth, I pounced her ass. I couldn't stand my brothers, but I didn't play about them period.

"That's right Yah-Yah! That bitch knocked my ribs over."

"Break this shit up!" I heard KJ say.

The next thing I know, they were pulling me off her. Aunt Sherita drugged her out the back gate by her hair and slammed it. She gestured for the DJ to cut the music back on, and it was back cracking.

"This family is filled with a bunch of silly motherfuckers. It's a damn shame we can't have one event where shit goes smoothly. Kaine, you ought to be ashamed of yourself for even fucking with trash like that. Milania is nine months pregnant, and the last thing she needs is to be under stress like this, and as for you, Yah-Yah. Stop always fighting when Kaine wants you to. He needs to handle his own fucking problems. If he kept his dick in the pants, he wouldn't have this problem. Y'all gone get enough of fucking with these low budget ass hoes who have no respect. If you gone cheat on your woman, get you a side bitch that knows her fucking place. Take Milania in the house. This shit don't make any sense! The bad part is that y'all bring this fucking drama to my sister's house."

Grandma Peaches was snapping, and I was shocked. It had been a minute since she weighed in on our shenanigans.

"Really, grandma?" Kaine said.

"Don't say shit to me, Kaine. Instead of questioning me about why I'm getting on your ass, go check on Milania with your stupid ass." Instead of Kaine checking on her, he went out of the gate instead.

"I told that nigga to stop fucking with that crazy bitch when he caught her riding pass the crib," Kash said as he passed the blunt to me that he was smoking.

"Well, I'm glad I did beat her ass then."

"He's gone have to murk that bitch," Kash said as he walked off. *That hoe must be bad for business,* I thought to myself.

Moments later, my parents walked in the gate. I put my blunt out and went to greet them. My father walked right past me as if I was invisible. That hurt like hell and had me on the brink of shedding tears.

"Give him some time, Yah-Yah. Plus, he knows you were just out here fighting like you had no sense. Let Kaine handle his own bullshit. That's the same girl I saw him with at the club, so he's been messing with that crazy bitch for some time now. I don't feel sorry for nobody but Milania. I love you, Yah-Yah. Start making better choices with how you handle things."

My mother walked off, and I just stood in the middle of the backyard completely lost. I was having a hard time understanding how my parents have never really had good judgment but passed judgment on us kids so easily. Over the years we have witnessed them doing so much crazy shit. They've done so much shit in front of us kids, and now we're grown, and they want us to behave in a way they never actually behaved. At the same time, I know they mean well and want us to be better than them. I was no longer in the mood to party after that, so I headed home. After about an hour or so, I was pulling into the driveway. I sat there for a minute before heading inside. Reality kicked in that I would be there alone. I immediately started to regret leaving the party. After sitting in the car for about thirty minutes, I went inside. Although I didn't want to face reality, I needed to get used to the fact that Yahmeen and I were no longer together. I was fooling myself because I'll never accept that shit.

It wasn't a good hour of me being home before my mom called and told me to get to the hospital because Milania ended up going into labor. She told me to try calling Kaine because no one could get in contact with him. On my way to the hospital, I tried calling him over and over again with no luck. Kaine better not had been with that bitch while Milania was giving birth to his son.

Chapter Eight

MILANIA

P issed wasn't a word for the way I was feeling. The last thing I
wanted to do was go in labor behind being stressed the fuck out.
The worse thing a nigga could ever do is stress his bitch out while she's
pregnant. The last thing I wanted to do was have another miscarriage.
The last time that shit happened was the worst time for me. Kaine
made life a living hell for me. The nigga was blaming me for some shit
that was beyond my control. Ever since that incident, we had been
good and had no issues. Ladybug had gotten so big, and Kaine was now
officially her daddy. She is now a Kenneth child, and I couldn't be
happier. His parents treat my baby like she has their blood running
through their veins. The best decision I've ever made was allowing
Kaine to be her father. Kaine has always taken care of us and made
sure we were straight. I've never had an issue with him cheating or
anything. That man comes homes every night like clockwork. He
answers the phone no matter what he's doing when I call. We are
always together, so that's why I was shocked at the events that transpired. I'm trying to figure out when this nigga had the time to cheat.

He had to be messing with the bitch for some time now. She had an
agenda showing up at his aunt's house. I had so many questions for his
motherfucking ass, but he was nowhere to be found.

"Did you talk to your brother yet?" I asked through another hard ass contraction.

The pain I was in had me ready to give in and ask for an epidural. Earlier in my pregnancy, I opted to deliver without drugs. That was only because when I gave birth to Ladybug, it was smooth sailing, not this time around though. This baby is kicking my ass.

"Nope, he still hasn't answered."

I was glad Yah-Yah and Ms. Tahari were here with me. The rest of the family had come and left. This baby was taking forever, and they were too impatient to wait. They were also all out looking for Kaine with his stupid ass. Besides being pissed at him, I was starting to worry because his phone was now going to voicemail. That wasn't like him not to answer his phone.

"Here eat some ice chips. I really think you should start leaning towards getting the epidural, Milania. There is no need for you to be sitting up here in all this pain when you can get something to ease it."

Ms. Tahari had been trying her best to convince me to get the epidural. I was so happy that she was here with me. She had been the closest thing I had to a mother in a really long time. As she placed a wet towel on my head, I grabbed the bed rails and braced myself for the next pain. I felt that shit coming, and it was the big one.

"I need Kaineeeee!" I cried out in agony. His deceit would be addressed later. Right now I needed the father of my child to be here while I go through this shit.

"Yah-Yah, get over here and keep her calm. Let me make some phone calls and see where the fuck he at. This shit reminds me of the time Thug almost missed me giving birth. Like father like god damn son. I'm sick of this shit." Ms. Tahari grabbed her phone and left out of the room.

"You think he's okay?"

"He's fine, Milania. Let's just focus on my nephew coming into this world healthy." She fed me some more ice chips and placed the wet towel on my forehead.

I was trying my best not to worry about Kaine or think about the shit that happened today. It was extremely hard though. The pains were kicking my ass, and I was indeed about to make the decision to get the epidural. I closed my eyes and tried my best to get through the pain. I silently prayed that Kaine would show up soon. If he's not dead or in jail, I'll never forgive him for missing the birth of our child.

§

"It's about time you woke up," Kaine said as he kissed my forehead.

My body felt so sore and heavy. For a minute I had to gather myself to see where I was. Then it came to me that I was in the hospital. I pulled the covers back and noticed my stomach was gone. I begin to panic like crazy.

"Where's my baby?"

"Calm down. The babies are fine." Kaine smiled like a Cheshire cat, but I was confused as hell.

"Babies?" I was lost because all of my pregnancy there was nothing but one baby on the ultrasound. How is it possible that they missed another baby?"

"You had twins boys. Are you ready to meet them?"

Ms. Tahari was so excited, but I for damn sure wasn't. I came in this motherfucker to have a baby, not two. I started overthinking like crazy. My ass only had shit at home for one damn baby. I know that we could go out and get all the things we needed, but at the same time, I wasn't prepared for two babies.

Kaine gently placed both of the babies in each of my arms, and I melted. They both looked just like Kaine. I was still in shock, but this was an amazing moment.

"Ladybug is going to go crazy when she meets them." They looked like little girls with all of the hair they had on their heads.

"Yes, she is. I already FaceTimed and showed her. Talking about she got two real Baby Alive dolls," Ms. Tahari said as she took pictures of us.

"What are we going to name them?" Kaine asked.

"Kaine and King Kenneth."

We had already agreed that we would name the baby Kaine Jr. when we were under the impression we were just having one. This surprise ass baby had to be named King. He was going to do big things in life. After all, he came into this world with a bang.

"I love it. Don't be over there feeling all bad and uncertain about the future. Trust me. This same thing happened to me. My ass thought I was pregnant with only one baby and came home with two babies. The shit is hereditary. Don't trip. You know we got you one hundred percent."

That's why I loved Ms. Tahari. She always made everything sound like it was going to be okay. I'm glad she's been through so much. I can take her advice and feel like it's genuine. It helps that she never condones her kids' bullshit. It's not often you can find a mother who doesn't always take up for her son.

"Where my grandboys at?" Thug came in with big blue teddy bears and the biggest smile on his face.

Looking over at Kaine, I could tell he was happy about finally being a father. I was absolutely elated about being the mother of his children. At the same time, we still had unfinished business. Right now, we can relish in the fact that we just had babies, but I can assure you he will come clean about that bitch.

❦

It had been three weeks since I gave birth and one week since I had been home from the hospital. After giving birth, I ended up having some complications that led to me hemorrhaging and unable to have any more kids. I had to have a full hysterectomy. Between giving birth to twins and no longer being able to have more children, I felt like I was losing my mind. The doctor says that I'm suffering from Post Partum Depression. I wouldn't wish this shit on my worse enemy. I'm in such a bad space mentally that I don't even want to deal with my children. Ms. Tahari decided we would move into her house temporarily so that she could help out. I feel so bad because it's like she and Thug are raising kids all over again.

Kaia, Kahari, and Kylie have been the biggest help. I don't have to lift a finger, and that feels good to have that support. At the same time,

I would love nothing more but to be in my own home getting adjusted to life with my babies. Kaine is not making the situation better. He acts like he's super irritated behind me being so emotionally disconnected. The nigga had been avoiding me like the plague since I made it home from the hospital. He would come in after being out all day, check on me, and then go sleep in another part of the house. I needed him more than ever, but of course, he was being selfish. Knowing him, he was blaming me for needing a damn hysterectomy. We still hadn't discussed the issue about the chick, and now I was more than ready. If he thought the shit was over because of my current state he was sadly mistaken. I stayed up on purpose for him to try and sneak his ass in the house.

"What you doing up? Are you okay?"

"I'm good. Let's talk about your side bitch, Kaine."

"Really, Milania? That's what you want to talk about?"

"Hell yeah! Nigga, you been avoiding the topic like the shit is going to go away. In case you forgotten a bitch showed up and acted a fool behind you. Your ass hasn't even addressed the situation, which lets me know it's some bullshit in the game. Now, who the fuck is she?" I had to raise my voice to let this stupid nigga know I was dead ass serious with his ass.

"Lower your voice. This is not the time or the place to be discussing that. Let's just focus on you getting better so that you can take care of our kids. You need to boss the fuck up and get on your shit. Bitches have babies every day and you walking around this motherfucker like giving birth to my kids is the end of the world. It doesn't help that you had to have a damn hysterectomy."

"Are you serious right now, Kaine?" I was in shock hearing him talk to me like that.

"I'm not trying to argue with you, Milania. Just get well so that we can go home. Let's talk about this some other time.

"You good. We ain't got shit to talk about, my nigga. When I do get well, you better hope that my kids and I come home to your evil ass."

I now understood why Yah-Yah snapped and burnt the damn house down. These niggas were way out of control with the harsh ass shit they say out of their mouths. Did Kaine really think he could speak to me that way and we would be cool? I think the fuck not.

"Don't ever think you can leave with my kids and you can live life peacefully. Take your meds because you're definitely losing your mind speaking some fuck shit like that." He walked out of the room, and at that moment, I knew I had to get it together.

It was crazy how all he wanted me to do was stay home while he ran the streets. He had even gone so far as to stop me from being a part of the Boss Ladies. He had the biggest fall out with Ka'Jairea. To keep the friction down, I decided just to steer clear of the Boss Ladies. I fucked up letting him dictate my life. That's cool though. I got a trick for his ass. Once I get my mind right, I'm back on my Boss Lady bullshit. My babies will not be a hindrance on me making my own way.

As I laid in the bed, I heard my babies crying, but I refused to get up. It was his turn to feed and change them. I placed a pillow over my head trying to drown them out, but it didn't help. Jumping up from the bed, I rushed to their nursery their granny had put together for them. I fed, changed them, and then they went back to sleep. It honestly felt good to take care of them. That was the most I had done since given birth. Heading back to the guest room that I had been staying in, I passed the room where Kaine was knocked out. I immediately became angry. His ass was not that knocked out that he didn't hear our boys crying. I wanted to beat his ass as he snored, but I came up with a better trick. I went to the bathroom and filled a bucket up with water. The nigga was on his back asleep which worked out good for me. I dumped the water right on his damn face. The nigga was flopping around on the bed like a roach that had just got sprayed with some roach spray. He jumped up and ran his ass dead smack into the wall.

"Ahhhh! What the fuck, Milania?"

"Stop fucking playing with me! You heard our kids crying, and you let them. Your ass be gone all day, so the least your black ass could do is come in and help out. Your ass is throwing around all these demands, but you're not doing anything to help out."

As I spoke, I was trying to keep my game face on but I couldn't his ass was drenched. All I could do was laugh, and that pissed him off. He tried to chase me, but I hauled ass getting back to the room that I was sleeping in and locked the door.

"I swear to God. I'm fucking you up, Milania!"

"Leave me alone you wet ass nigga!" I climbed in bed and had the biggest smile ever. It felt good to do something spiteful to his ass since he's been sitting around doing shit to me.

The next morning I woke in such a good headspace. I immediately wanted to run and check on my babies. To my surprise, Kaine was already in the nursery feeding and changed them. Had I known trying to drown the bitch in his sleep would make him help out, I would have been done the shit. It warmed my heart seeing him with the twins. King started to cry, so I walked in and took him out of Kaine's arms. He looked like he was struggling trying to cradle them.

"I'm sorry for throwing the water on you last night."

The last thing I wanted to do was apologize, but I decided to take the high road. All I want is peace and tranquility in our relationship. For the most part, there is still the elephant in the room that needs to be addressed. I prefer sooner than later. Kaine needs to come clean with me before I find out on my own. The consequences will definitely be far worse than had he manned up and clean. In the meantime, I'm going to get on my shit and take care of my kids. Fuck this Post Partum Depression shit. It's getting the best of me, and I'm much stronger than that.

"I'm sorry for the way I acted, and I promise to help out more. Shit has been hectic out in the streets. I'll make sure when the time is right we will have that discussion about the chick that came to the party. In the meantime, promise me you'll get better so that you can take care of our kids."

I stared into his eyes as he spoke, and his words were genuine. Honestly, I wasn't content with him not immediately telling me about this situation with this bitch. In my opinion, it was something serious, and he was too afraid to tell me. He should absolutely be scared, but I'll let him make it for the time being. I just wanted to love on all three of my babies. Life for me has drastically changed. I went from being the mother of one to a mother of three overnight.

"I promise I'll get better." He pulled me in close, and we engaged in a deep kiss.

"Let me get out of here. I need to meet up with KJ and Kash to survey a building that we're trying to buy. Just call me if you need me."

After exchanging another kiss, Kaine left. Enjoying the bonding time I was having with my sons, I decided to take them back to my room.

"I'm so glad to see you're tending to them," Ms. Tahari said as she came inside of the room and placed some clean linen at the foot of the bed.

"I've come to the conclusion that I'm stronger than the Post Partum Depression. I can't let that block me from bonding with my babies. Plus, Kaine is ready for us to go home with the kids."

"Fuck what Kaine is talking about. He doesn't understand what women go through after giving birth. He's just like his stupid ass daddy back in the day. Thug would have my ass pregnant damn near every six months and be mad when I was tired of that shit. I swear out of all my boys I see Thug in Kaine the most. That's why I really came in here to talk to you. When I see you, I see so much of me at your age. I had no family besides my grandma. When she passed that left me with Thug and Momma Peaches. She was always good to me, but she loved her sons. At the same time, she always put Barbie and me on game in regards to how to handle her sons. She spoke to us from a woman's standpoint and not a mother's. I do the same thing with all my daughters-in-law. I feel like I owe it to you all because you girls are dealing with my sons. I'm a mother second, but a woman first. Don't let Kaine knock you off your square with his bullshit. No matter what you do, don't ever lose yourself in him. Never let him dim your light so that he can shine brighter. What I'm saying is live your life too. Whatever you want to do to better yourself, then do it.

If you want to run your own business, then launch it. If you want to get your hands dirty in the family business, then do that. I started Boss Lady Inc. with my crew. We were all holding our niggas down to the fullest, but they wanted us to be stay at home moms. At the same time our husbands were out taking penitentiary risks and throwing rocks at the cemetery, and that's where we stepped in. In this thug life, sometimes you have to get your hands dirty after making breakfast for your children. Hell, sometimes you may have to tuck them in and then go get your hands dirty. It's all about what you're willing to lose and what you're willing to sacrifice so that you don't lose. You can either be his Bonnie or the bored bitch he dreads coming home to.

Now don't get me wrong because whether you're a stay at home type of woman or a ride or die chick, a man is going to do what he wants to do. It took Thug and me years to get it together where we had common ground. To this day, we still have fights or arguments about the littlest things. I'm consistently reminding him of my place in his life and what I've sacrificed for him. In the beginning, I let Thug run all over me. I had to put my foot down, a bullet in his ass, and kill a couple of bitches. You have to do what you have to do, Milania. Don't let Kaine run all over you, and never let a bitch destroy your family." She winked her eye at me and walked out of the bedroom.

I heard her loud and very clear. It didn't take a rocket scientist to catch on to the wisdom she was speaking. It was imperative that I stepped my game up, or Kaine would think he could always do what the fuck he wanted.

Chapter Nine

KAINE

This bitch Kionni was going to make me murk her loose pussy ass. For the longest, I had been putting the bitch off and keeping her at arm's length. Granted at one point, she was my faithful side bitch, but of course, she caught main bitch feelings, so I needed to cut her ass the fuck off. I should have known she was a crazy bitch from the way she liked me to choke her when I fucked her. I'm not going to lie. The bitch had some superb pussy and some sensational head. All that shit meant nothing at this point because she was bat shit crazy behind my ass. One would think after Yah-Yah whooped her ass that she would be done with her shit, but that only made her go harder. Now she's claiming to be pregnant, and that's the last thing I need. I'm not about to lose my family behind a bitch that means nothing to me.

"I can't believe you're doing this to me, Kaine!"

"Bitch shut the fuck up with all that crying and piss on the stick! What you thought you were just going to tell me you were pregnant and that was it? Piss on the stick before I beat your ass until you piss on yourself. I'm done playing these bitch ass games with you, Kionni!"

She was sitting on the toilet crying, and I didn't give a fuck.

"Okay! I lied, Kaine! I needed to tell you something so that you can come over here. It's been over a month, and you haven't even called to check on me. It's like you love her more than you love me. I just don't understand. We've been dealing with each other for over a year. Things were cool then all of a sudden you just switched up on me."

I wanted to smack some sense into this bitch, but I had to handle this shit differently.

"Clean yourself up and come out front." I headed into the living room to wait for her nutty ass to come out.

This is what I get for being greedy. Milania is everything a nigga wants, and I have no excuse as to why I fuck other bitches from time to time. I just do. The real nigga I am don't feel like I need to give an explanation for the shit either. It is what the fuck it is.

"Please don't be mad at me, Kaine! I love you so much."

"You don't love me Kionni because I don't love you. We just fucked a couple of times, and we had fun. You knew I had a girl from the jump. I never even gave you the impression that I was going to leave her for you. Let me ask you some real shit.

"Have I ever spent the night with you?"

"No."

"Have I ever took you out on romantic dates?"

"No."

"Exactly. I've never wined and dined you. I've never laid up in your crib. All we do is smoke and fuck at the hotel, not to mention you help me do a lot of business runs. You get bread off that shit though. You showing up at my auntie's crib was out of line, ma. It's a must I caught you off. You're bad for business and extremely detrimental to my relationship. I'm sorry Kionni, but we're done."

"I can't believe this! You're sitting here acting like we just met. We used to fuck under the bleachers all the time in high school."

"Really, Kionni? I used to fuck you and all of your friends in high school. Let the shit go. As I said, we're done. Stay the fuck away from me, and if I catch you anywhere around my family, I'll put a bullet in your fucking head."

I hurried up and got the fuck out of her crib. That bitch had lost what little mind she had left. I honestly had forgotten all about fucking her and her crew back in high school. As I drove off, my dick got hard thinking about their freaky, young asses. Her ass disappeared after sophomore year and just last year I ran into her ass. Had I known she was dick silly, I would have never fucked with her again. I hope and pray her crazy ass gets the picture and stay the fuck away from me.

I should have been heading back home, but I wanted to check on Yah-Yah. Although she's the one that's quick to pop off when shit gets hectic, I know she's having a hard time with this breakup. Out of my siblings, I love me some Yah-Yah. That was my baby when we were kids. I used to straight send her off to do shit, and she used to do it too. Pops would never whoop her, but Kash and I would get it. We were some badass twins, and we're the reason why Yah-Yah is the way she is. She's so used to being a badass that she doesn't know when it's okay to fold. I guess none of Kenneth children do. I guess we wait for something drastic to happen before its time to get our shit together. This situation with Kionni has definitely scared my ass straight. I'm taking my ass home to my family no matter what.

§

About an hour later, I was pulling into Yah-Yah's driveway. I didn't see her car, so I wasn't sure she was even home. Before I could even get out of the car, she was standing outside on her front porch. She had her son on her hip looking like a ghetto queen for real. It's still unbelievable that she's a mother.

"What you doing over here? Your ass better start calling first. I almost came out and started blasting your ass, my nigga."

"What I can't come and see my favorite sister in the whole wide world?"

"Hell yeah, you can! Just call first." I kissed her on the cheek, and then we headed inside the house.

"Damn Yah, this bitch is laid the fuck out!"

I walked around looking at her new crib and wondered what type of kryptonite her ass had to make that nigga buy her a house after she burned down the first one. Lord knows if it were me, her ass would have been sleeping on a cot at the homeless shelter.

"It's not all the way together, but it is dope as hell. You want something to drink?"

"Yeah, give me a double shot of Rémy with ice."

"Nigga, do I look like a bartender? You better make that shit yourself. Let me go lay him down. I'll be right back."

"Your ass is rude as fuck. This my first time at your crib and you not being hospitable!"

"Nigga, please!" She waved me off and walked up the spiral staircase.

Looking around, I had to admit that Yahmeen had done his thing with this motherfucking crib. He had to love Yah-Yah to take care of her the way he does after all of her shit. Heading over to her fully stocked bar, I poured my drink and took a seat.

"Now what the hell brings you over here? Milania must have finally put your ass out for fucking with her." She laughed as she poured herself some wine and sat next to me at the bar.

"Milania and I are good. I fucked up though by fucking that crazy ass girl Kionni. You might not remember her, but we went to high school with her. We used to run trains on her and friends. Her ass disappeared all of a sudden, and it wasn't until last year that we crossed paths again. I should never have started back fucking with that bitch. Her ass is nutty as hell. I just had to let her ass know that we were over and done with. That shit she pulled at Aunt Sherita's house was the end of us. That added with the bitch trying to play like she was pregnant. I cornered that bitch at her crib in the bathroom and tried to make her piss on the stick in front of me. Her ass had to come clean and say she was lying to a nigga. I definitely had to cut that bitch off."

"You sure that bitch gone leave you alone that easy? Maybe I should go pay that hoe a visit to make sure she does. You can't trust these unstable dick silly ass bitches, bro." She knocked back her shot of wine and poured her another glass.

I thought in my mind if I could trust that she would just go on ahead about her business, but that hoe knows not to play with me. period. She had the fear of God in her eyes when I told her that I would put a bullet in her head.

"Nah, sis! That bitch ain't crazy. In the meantime, what's going on with you and Yahmeen?"

"Nothing. We're not together anymore, but he's a good provider and an even better father. "I could sense a hint of sadness even though she was trying to hide it.

"Yahmeen is cool and all but, I'll murk him if you want me to." I knocked back my shot and waited for her to respond.

"Hell no!" She laughed, but I was serious as hell.

"I'm serious as fuck. You know I love you more than anything in this world. I'll murder anybody that fuck with you. Just give me the word, and I'll handle it. At the same time, I know shit is hard on you as far as you him not being together. If you love that man, then try and make it right. It's okay to go after what you want. I'm taking my ass home right now and make shit right with Milania. I love her, and the last thing I want to do is lose her to some bullshit. If you truly want to be that man's wife, let him know. I'm a nigga, and I know that's exactly what he wants. You're strong as hell, but a little too strong for him. Let him lead, Yah-Yah. It's okay to let him lead. I love you, lil sis. I just wanted to check on you and make sure that you were okay. Let me get out of here so that I can spend some time with Milania and the kids. Promise me you'll talk to him."

"I promise, bro. Now go ahead and chill with your family. Don't hesitate to reach out if you need me to handle that bitch."

We hugged one another, and I headed home. During the drive, I prayed Yah-Yah took heed to what I was saying. That man loves Yah-Yah. She just needs to let him love her.

Chapter Ten

YAH-YAH

It had been a week since Kaine had come over and had the heart to heart talk with me. Ever since his visit, I've been thinking and thinking about what to do or say to Yahmeen. We've been in contact in regards to our son, but anything else is not discussed. I'm starting to think he will never want to get back with me. When he comes to pick up our son or drop him off, he doesn't even come inside of the house. Now I know how baby mommas get treated when they baby daddy can't stand their ass. I believe that's how Yahmeen feels about me these days. He doesn't like me at all. He only tolerates me because we share a child.

I've put a lot of thought into talking to Yahmeen about the way that I feel. All I keep thinking about is if he rejects me again. The last time I burnt the damn house down, so I have no control over what I will do this time around. My crazy ass may want to take Kaine up on his offer to murk the nigga. At the same time, I know that I can't do that. I love that man, and the last thing I would ever do is take my son's father away from him. This would be the time I would have to grow the fuck up and not allow my emotions to get the best of me. I would absolutely show my parents that I can be levelheaded and not act on impulse all of the time. I love Yahmeen, but I have to accept the fact that if it's over, then it's over.

"Are you sure you want to do this, Yah-Yah?" Heaven asked as she passed me the blunt that we had been smoking.

"Yes, I have to try and get my nigga back. I never thought I would miss him the way that I have, but I do. Lord, all I want is to get married like we planned and live happily ever after."

Heaven and I were headed over to his parent's house, unannounced of course. She had overheard Yasir speaking about some big party they were having today. I didn't care if they were having a family function. If I needed to confess how much I loved him to the world, then I definitely would.

"Well, I'm with whatever you're with. Sometimes I might not agree with the way you handle things, but I'm riding with your ass until the wheels fall off. Let's go get your nigga!" Heaven and I laughed, and I continued to drive towards his parent's house in deep thought.

I never allowed negative things to enter my mind because I didn't want it to manifest. Just thinking about what I was about to do had me feeling proud of my self. Had my father and I been on talking terms, he would have been the first person I called to tell him what I was doing. I was still so hurt behind my father and I not being in a good place that I would cry at the very thought of him. No matter what, I know my daddy loves me. He just wants to show me some type of tough love for a change. In the beginning, I was mad, but I know he's only doing it out of love and to also teach me a lesson. Between him and Yahmeen teaching me lessons, I'm about to go crazy. At the same, they have both made me learn my lesson in the hardest of ways.

"Damn! It's a lot of people here," I spoke nervously.

"Don't chicken out on me now. Plus, Jr. is here so that can be the reason you came over."

"I'm not, Heaven. Let's get this shit over with."

I turned the car off and let out a deep breath before getting out of the car. I was nervous as hell as I walked up to the door. My ass was happy that Heaven was with me because I for damn sure couldn't do it by myself. The party was in the backyard area, so we headed through the back gate. I stopped in my tracks looking at what looked like

Yahmeen was down on one knee in front of the same bitch he claimed to not fuck with like that. I immediately walked over and snatched my son out of his mother's arms. Yahmeen was looking like a deer in headlights.

"Really, you're proposing to this bitch?" I snatched the ring out of his fucking hand.

"Stop it, Yah-Yah!" He tried grabbing and pushing me out of the backyard, but I wasn't moving.

"Get your motherfucking hands off of me! You got my son here while you're proposing to this bitch.

"Please leave this house with that nasty foul mouth!" his father said.

"Fuck you and this house!"

"I got this dad! Let me handle Yah-Yah!" Yahmeen said to his father as he continued to push me towards the gate.

"You have no handle of this situation. This is why this family will never accept her. Remove her from the property, or I will have her physically removed.

"I wish the fuck you would even think about putting your hands on me. My father will air this bitch out, and you know it!"

I handed Heaven my son and turned around to beat the bitch Raja up. She had a smirk on her face, and I caught it. There was nothing funny about this situation. So since she wanted to laugh, I decided to give the bitch something to cry about it.

"Let her go, Yah-Yah!" Yahmeen said with one big jerk that made me let her go.

I looked around at all of his Arabic family staring at me like I was an animal. This nigga was making me act crazy, not to mention bringing out the worse in me. In that moment, hurt took over, and the anger subsided. Yahmeen grabbed me by my waist and carried me out of the backyard.

"This is absolutely unacceptable Yahmeen!" A big man started to yell after us, but I saw Yasir step in front of him to keep him from walking towards us.

"Why are you doing this to me?" I cried.

"Calm down, Ka'Jaiyah! I need you to go home right now! I'll be there in a little while. Just please don't do this. That female you just attacked is the daughter of one of the most ruthless kingpin's in the world!"

"I don't give a fuck about her or her father! Do you know who my father is? Or, did your ass forget. Damn, Yahmeen, that bitch means that much to you?"

"Of course I know who your father is. It's because I know who he is that I'm telling you to go home. We aren't together anymore, Yah-Yah! Whatever I do now is none of your business! As long as your bills are paid and my son straight that's all that matters. Go home right now!" He slightly pushed me away, but at the same time, he couldn't even look at me as he spoke.

"We were just engaged a minute ago, and you're already proposing to someone else. Am I that bad? You've moved on like what we had never meant anything! Why, Yahmeen? Just tell me whyyyy!" I had never in my life cried so hard. My heart was aching so bad, and I felt like I would have a heart attack.

"Come on, sis. Let me take you home." Yasir grabbed me as Yahmeen quickly walked off.

"Yahmeen! Yahmeen! Say something please! Don't do this!" Yasir managed to pick me up and place me into the passenger seat of the car. Heaven placed my son in his car seat and jumped in the driver seat. I was so blinded with tears that my vision was blurry.

"Don't cry, Yah-Yah! He's making the worst decision of his life." Heaven's voice cracked as she tried to console me.

"I fucked up so bad, and he doesn't want me at all! How could he do that to me?" I cried, and Heaven pull me over to her let me lay her head on my shoulder.

I cried so hard that I got a migraine. All I wanted to do was go home and go to sleep. The worst part of it all was that I never wanted to wake up from this fucking nightmare.

"Stop crying, Yah-Yah! Everything is going to be okay. I swear to God you need to tell your brothers so that they can beat his ass. No, tell Uncle Thug so he can torture his ass."

"I don't want them to know. Promise me you won't tell them this. I don't want anyone to know this shit just happened. They will absolutely kill him, and I don't want to raise my son without a father. Just take me home."

"Don't worry I got you."

As she headed towards my house, it started to rain, and that shit made me cry harder. I knew that I had done some fucked up shit during our relationship, but I never thought it would lead to this. When Heaven dropped me off, she wanted to take Jr. home with her, but I needed him to be with me. Lying in bed that night, I cradled my son, and I promised myself that today was the last day I would cry over Yahmeen. If he wanted to marry someone else, then so be it. We weren't meant to be anyway if he chooses her like I never mattered.

The events of the day made me want to call my mother and tell her. I was in need of some Boss Lady wisdom. At the same time, I didn't need her shooting Yahmeen the fuck up. I think she would do it quicker than my daddy would. A hug was well needed from my daddy, but I needed to be a grown woman about this shit. I couldn't go running to my family when people don't do what I want them to do. I pushed Yahmeen away, and I have to deal with the fact that he doesn't want me anymore. I'm in the prime of my life and one of the baddest bitches walking around. It might hurt now, but I'm making a promise to myself this shit won't hurt in the long run. I'll be able to look at Yahmeen like he's just the father of my child and nothing more.

The sound of someone banging on my front door irritated the fuck out of me. I had cut my phone off and logged out of my social media. At the moment, I just wanted to be under the radar trying to get myself together. I acted as if nothing was wrong when my mother came and picked my son up. She is nosey as hell though, so I'm sure she could feel it. It had been a little over a week since the incident with Yahmeen, and I had completely shut down. Everybody had been calling me, including Yahmeen, but I didn't want to talk to anyone. His ass was the last person I wanted to talk to anyway.

Jumping up from my bed, I walked fast as hell getting to the front door. Without seeing who it was, I yanked the door open. To my surprise, it was Yahmeen's father and his assistant, which happens to be a man. In my heart of hearts, I believe these niggas be fucking. They're just way too close for me. This is surprising for him to even be on my doorstep. He had never come to our home so him being here is definitely a shock.

"May I help you?" I leaned against the doorframe looking a hot ass mess, but I could care less. I was well aware that he didn't care for me, and I for damn sure don't care about him.

"It's imperative we speak. Can I come in please?"

He had a serious look on his face and it kind of worried me. Hesitantly, I stepped to the side and allowed them to come in. I immediately regretted it because this nigga had some fucked up energy, and I didn't need it fucking up my house. I was going to sage the shit out of it when he left.

"What's so important that we have to speak? Is Yahmeen okay?"

"He is fine, but I'm here to give you this." His boyfriend handed me the thick duffle bag that he was carrying. I opened it, and it was filled to capacity with money.

"What is this for?" I grabbed a stack and thumbed through it before tossing it back

"That's five hundred thousand dollars to stay away from my son. He's about to embark on a business deal of a lifetime that will solidify his place in my organization. As you know, he's getting ready to be married to a very important woman, so it would be in your best interest to steer clear from my son if you get my drift."

This motherfucker had lost his mind. I had to pinch the bridge of my nose to keep from jumping across the coffee table and beating his old ass.

"Is that all he's worth? That man came from your loins, and all he's worth is a measly five hundred thousand dollars. It's crazy you think so low of me that you would ever offer me some money to leave the man alone. In my eyes, he's priceless. I don't give a fuck if he married a bitch while we're still together, no amount of money would make me ever not be in the life of my child's father. Let me guess you forgot we share a son."

He laughed, and I found myself sticking my hand inside the couch cushion to grab my gun. This old ass nigga was really trying me.

"How could I forget you have a son with him? I've hated it the moment I learned about it. I've grown to love him. That's why my wife and I would love for you to turn over your parental rights. You're a mentally unstable woman, and you are in no position to raise a child." That was it this man had pushed me too fucking far.

"Get the fuck out of my house before I put a bullet in your fucking head. Let me make myself perfectly clear. I am very mentally unstable! Don't fuck with me! My son is off limits to you and your wife going forward. If you even think about looking at him too long, I'll kill you and her stupid ass.

"Do you know what you're fucking with?"

"Obviously, you don't know who you're fucking with. Did you forget who the fuck I am and whose blood runs through my veins? If you love life, you'll start moving faster. Leave the bag for my pain and suffering."

I cocked my gun and smirked evilly at his ass. This motherfucker had just ignited a fire inside of me that I never knew was there. He and his boyfriend quickly got the hell out of dodge. I immediately called my mother to check on my son. I knew he was fine. It was just my motherly instinct that made me check on him. Angry wasn't even a word to describe the way that I was feeling. I was torn between calling Yahmeen and my father. His father was a snake, and for some reason, I deeply felt like he could hurt Yahmeen if the price were right. The shit had me going crazy, and I needed to talk to somebody about this shit, but not my parents. If I tell them this shit, it will be a war and carnage across the city.

At the end of the day, Yahmeen and I still share a son. This shit is so fucked up. Why would this man come to my home and do some fucked up shit like this? After smoking about two blunts to the face, I got dressed and headed over to Ka'Jairea house. It had been a minute since I went to my sister for advice. Kaine is the one out of my siblings that I talk about my problems to, but I can't tell that trigger happy nigga this. He'll fuck around and kill Yahmeen, Yasir, and their damn parents. Yeah, my big sis is the only person I could go to with this.

It was so funny looking at Ka'Jairea walking around her house in red bottoms and a silk robe. This girl looked just like our momma. I swear I was trying my best not to laugh at her ass, but she was showing the fuck out. My ass was high as a kite, so the shit was even funnier.

"What the fuck you laughing at?"

"I'm laughing at your ass."

"Do I amuse you bitch? Am I a clown or something?"

"Hell yeah, your ass is a clown. Your ass is walking around here looking just like Boss Lady. You got your red bottoms and your robe on. I swear that's how Ma be walking around the house all day. Daddy be loving that shit too."

"Hell yeah! That lady taught me everything about keeping my nigga satisfied. I am not the bitch that's about to be walking around in an ugly ass nightgown with a bonnet on. Niggas don't like that shit. It's unattractive as fuck. Plus, I'm a rich bitch and all my husband and I do is have rich sex. Your ass better take some notes so that you and Yahmeen can keep your shit together."

"Yahmeen and I are no longer together, and you know that." I rolled my eyes at her ass and flamed up another blunt.

"I know that, but right now y'all just taking a break. Your ass burnt that man house to the ground, and he's pissed right now. Yahmeen just needs some time."

"He needs so much time that he's about to get married to someone else!" Her eyes widened like saucers.

"What the fuck you mean he's getting married to someone else?"

"That's why I needed to talk to you. About two weeks ago, I went to Yahmeen's parents' house to make shit right with him. I basically walked in on his engagement to the bitch named Raja. She's supposed to be the daughter of his father's business partner. He was at the club the night that I burnt the house down with this same bitch. That nigga lied to my fucking face. To make matters worse, his father comes to the house today and offers me money to stay away from Yahmeen. The nigga even went so far to suggest that I turn my parental rights over. Before I knew it, I had upped on his ass and put the bitch out of my house. I made sure to take that money though."

"You should have killed his ass! Did you tell daddy what that fuck nigga did?"

"No! You better not tell him either. I'm going to handle this shit on my own. I haven't even said shit to Yahmeen about that. Honestly, I don't know what to do. What do you suggest?"

"I think not telling Daddy or Ma is a mistake because when they find out, they're going to go off. That nigga would be dead right now if you had told them. You know they don't play behind us. At the same time, I understand you wanting to handle some shit on your own. That's why you got me. Plus, your ass is technically a part of Boss Lady Inc., so it's time you put in work. All that walking around here throwing temper tantrums acting like a bitch is over. Let me tell you something. The last time I let a bitch think she could have Hassan was the last time. Don't sit back and let a bitch think she can have a nigga you put in work with. Hassan ass knows it's until death do us part, and I mean that shit. It's time you show that shit to Yahmeen. All you've shown that nigga is that your ass is spoiled ass bitch. It's time you show him you're not the bitch to be fucked with. Besides showing Yahmeen who the fuck you are, it's time to show our parents. We are the products of two of the most feared people in the city. Every day of our lives we have a point to prove. Get your shit together, Yah-Yah! I'm going to tell you like Ma told me. Kill any and everything that gets in the way of your happiness. Now, if you don't mind, I need to go make love to my husband before he hits the streets." She winked her eye at me and switched her ass up the spiral staircase.

I just shook my head as "Honey Love" by R. Kelly started blasting throughout the house. I grabbed my shit quick and got the hell out of there.

As I drove around aimlessly, the conversation between Ka'Jairea and me played over and over in my head. On the one hand, I knew I needed to tell my parents. On the other hand, I really needed to handle this on my own. I would call on my family in the event I needed them. In the meantime, I had every intention of putting my family back together. Yahmeen had no idea his father was a snake, but I was about to let his ass know. Come to think of it. I really needed to find out just who the fuck this bitch Raja was.

Once I made it home, I grabbed a bottle of wine and started doing a thorough search on the bitch. This bitch basically lived on IG. Going through her pictures made me angry. She had so many pictures of her and Yahmeen. The shit was truly legit with them. I became sick to my stomach because I never wanted to see him give love to any other woman but me. Seeing their wedding invitation angered me, but also gave me the location of the event. Raja made a big mistake by always posting her location. I now know that she's being fitted for her dress today. I felt like a crazy bitch as I rubbed my hands together like Bird Man.

As I headed upstairs to change, a text came through from my momma. She was letting me know that Yahmeen had just come and picked our son up, which was cool with me. If he had our son, that left me more time with his bitch.

᠅

I had been sitting inside of this bitch's condo for the last two hours and still she hadn't shown up. Thank God my Uncle Malik taught me how to pick locks when I was younger. It was a breeze getting inside this hoe's house. Looking around, I had to give it to her. The bitch had taste. Her condo didn't have shit on my crib though. I'll give the bitch an "A" for effort though. I decided to cut my phone off in the event someone would call me. I didn't need any distractions for what I was about to do. As I chilled on her sofa, thoughts of my son crossed my mind. I was doing this shit to give my son the same life my parents gave me, and I would do anything for my baby boy. Hearing her place her keys inside of the door I sat up quickly.

"What the hell are you doing in my house?" She went to grab her phone, but I quickly aimed my gun at her.

"No need for all of that! Come on in and have a seat." I gestured for her to toss her phone towards me.

"I understand that you're mad about Yahmeen choosing me, but I have no control over that. Maybe you should rethink the way you handle things. Do you think he wants to marry someone like you? It's a reason why he chose me."

She sat down on the sofa and crossed her legs.

"I'm exactly who he wants to marry. Don't get it twisted bitch! His father chose you. You're nothing but a cash cow. That's actually why I'm here. You see his father stopped by to see me and offered me a significant amount of cash to stay away from him. I took the money because I got this bright idea to offer you the money." She caught me off because she started to laugh at me. The bitch thought this was a game.

"There is no amount of money in the world worth me giving up Yahmeen. That's what you were about to say right? See, I've been promised to Yahmeen from birth. He rightfully belongs to me. You, American women, feel so entitled to our men. I don't care if Yahmeen was raised here. He has Middle Eastern blood running through his veins. So, you see, it's only right we keep the bloodline going. Did he tell you that we're expecting? Is that why you're here showing your jealous side?"

"This is not jealousy. Bitch, this is me offering you an outlet to keep your life. Now let me make you an offer you shouldn't refuse. Take this five hundred thousand and walk away."

I was not playing, and this was my last offer to the bitch. Her constant talking was making my trigger finger itch.

"Why would I take five hundred thousand when I'm worth millions!" She smirked and leaned forward to stare into my eyes.

This bitch was trying to call my bluff. Without even thinking about it, I pulled the trigger and shot her right in the middle of the forehead. The way the blood shot out the back of her head made me queasy. From the moment I decided to go to the bitch's crib, I knew I was going to murk her ass. I was trying to prolong it to get more information out of her, but she just couldn't stop talking about shit I didn't want to hear. I knew for a fact I was killing the bitch when she said she was pregnant. I would never co-exist in this world with another bitch that had a baby with Yahmeen. Stepping over her body, I made sure to leave without touching anything.

. . .

About an hour later, I stood underneath the shower and let the water-fall all over my body. Murking somebody seems easy when you pull the trigger, and in a way, it is. It's seeing their cold, dead eyes afterwards that's the problem. After drying off, I climbed in bed and stared at the ceiling. I couldn't believe I had killed this bitch. Out of the blue, I remembered that I had shut my phone off. Reaching over on the night-stand, I powered it on. Texts immediately started to come through. They were mainly from my mom trying to get in contact with me. She was worried because I hadn't answered. Quickly I shot a text back letting her know I was good. Staring at the ceiling, I mentally prepared for the war that was sure to come, but I was ready for whatever. At least I can sleep comfortably knowing she'll never be with Yahmeen again.

Chapter Eleven

YAHMEEN

Learning that Raja was pregnant was not a part of my plan. It was bad enough I was agreeing to marry the bitch to throw my father off. I had to fuck her in order to make the shit real. I just didn't count on this bitch poking holes in the condom. One thing about me is I stay ten steps ahead of motherfuckers, especially when it concerns me. From the jump I've always felt like this bitch had ulterior motives. Around her father, she pretended to be this innocent ass girl, but around me, she portrayed herself to be the heiress of her father's empire.

Somewhere down the line, Raja had created an agenda of her own. While I was using her as a pawn in my plans to take over, she was using me as a pawn in hers. She made sure to act like that wasn't what she wanted around me. In fact, she went out of her way to prove how much better she was for me than Yah-Yah. How could she ever love me, and she knew nothing about a nigga? The bitch moved too suspect for me, so I planted devices in her car and inside of her condo. That's how I found out the bitch poked holes in the condom and was plotting to take over the entire time. I planned to marry the bitch and trick her out of her daddy out of his bricks. My father had already given me exactly what I needed to take over. All he wanted was for me to marry

Raja. He was hell-bent on it. I wasn't sure what her father had over my father. Whatever it was it had to be serious enough to make him try to pay Yah-Yah off to stop fucking with me. It was a good thing I put them cameras in her condo or I wouldn't know that.

Imagine my surprise when I get an alert to my phone about movement in Raja's house. Watching Yah-Yah's crazy ass in action threw me for a loop. I never thought she was really going to pull the trigger. I just thought she was trying to scare her but seeing Yah-Yah murk Raja without a second thought. The shit had me fucked up.

I immediately went into panic mode. Yah-Yah had just started a war, and we were directly in the middle of it. I just hope she didn't hesitate when shit got real out in the field. Without alerting her, I dropped our son back off to her parents. I needed to get to her immediately before she did anything else that was reckless and dangerous.

§♠

"What are you doing here? Where is Jr.?" Yah-Yah was shocked to see me standing at the foot of her bed. Her ass had dozed off and was sleeping like a baby. Instead of waking her up, I sat at the foot of the bed and flamed up a blunt.

"Don't worry about Jr. He's good, ma. I'm more worried about you." I blew smoke in the air and stared at her.

She hopped out of bed and went into the bathroom. I could tell that she was nervous as ever as she threw water in her face and rinsed her mouth. I also took notice of the fact that she was naked as ever. It had been a minute since I saw her body. Thick wasn't even a word to describe her. I observed her pretty white toes, and she came back into the room. She sat on the other side of the bed far away from me. She was trying her best to hide her nervousness, so I decided to apply pressure. Standing to my feet, I walked over and stood directly in front of her.

"What, Yahmeen?"

"Don't what me. You didn't hear me say I'm worried about you." I gently lifted her head so that she could look at me as I spoke.

"There is no need to worry about me. I'm no longer your problem.

You dumped me remember, and if memory serves me right, you're about to get married to another woman." Yah-Yah smirked with her sneaky. *Lord, why do I love this crazy ass woman?*

"Do you love me, Ka'Jaiyah Kenneth?" I parted her legs so that I could stand in between them.

"Of course I love you." She tried to look away, but I tightened my grip on her chin. I needed her to look directly in my eyes when she answered my questions.

"Would you kill for me?" I rubbed my thumb back and forth across her lips. She was starting to tense up, so I needed to relax her.

"Without a doubt." With my free hand, I cupped her left breast, which made her jump at my touch.

"Why would you kill for me?"

"Because I know that you would do the same for me."

I was now cupping her right breast as I gently tugged on her nipple. She moaned, and I gently pushed her back on the bed. She moaned louder as I opened her legs and softly rubbed my fingers across her clit.

"I have a feeling there's about to be a war. Would you go to war with me, Ka'Jaiyah?"

She was soaking wet, so I was able to insert two fingers inside of her. I gently found the spot that I've come to love so much. Feeling her juices made me rock up. It had been a minute since I felt her.

"Yesssssss, Yahmeen! I'd go to war with you!" she yelled out in pleasure.

My intentions were to come over here and get down to the bottom of the situation, but seeing her naked made me change plans. A nigga needed to be inside of Yah-Yah. It had been a minute since I had been inside of the pussy that I owned outright. It's always the pretty and crazy bitches that have the best pussy. I let my jogging pants drop to the floor, and without hesitation, I roughly flipped Yah-Yah over. I slid my dick in full speed and went in.

"Ahhhhh, waitttt! Yahmeen!"

"Shut the fuck up and take this dick! You ready for me to come back home!"

"Yassssss!"

"You gone be a good girl and listen to me." She was trying her best to push me back, but I knocked her hands away. Yah-Yah was about to feel all this dick.

"Yassss! I swear I'll be a good girl! It hurts, Yahmeen! Slow down!" she whined.

"Tell me you love this gangsta dick!" I sped up because I felt myself getting ready to release.

"Oh my god! Yasssss! I love that gangsta dick. Don't stop, Yahmeen! I'm about to cum all over that gangsta dick!" I looked down, and Yah-Yah had my dick covered in her juices. That add with her fat ass bouncing everywhere had me releasing all my seeds deep inside of her. I prayed that I popped her ass off.

"Fuckkk!" I grunted as her pussy sucked me dry.

Yah-Yah fell flat on the bed, and I fell beside her. My phone was going off like crazy, but I already knew it was my father. He would have to wait. I have more pressing issues on my hand like getting her ass to understand what the hell was about to pop off. I sat up and flamed my blunt back up. Looking over my shoulder, I noticed that Yah-Yah had her back turned to me. I could have sworn I heard her sniffling but not her big badass. She just murked a bitch in cold blood, so I wasn't buying that shit. Instead of trying to see if she was crying, I decided to call her bluff.

"I'm about to go ahead and get up out of here. I'll leave some money on the dresser so that you can go shopping tomorrow. I'm going to go pick up Jr. and then head to the crib. Getting out of the bed, I never saw the bed lamp coming my way until it crashed into the wall behind me.

"Really nigga! You come over here and fuck me like that, only to think you about to go home to that bitch! Well, take your stupid ass home to that bitch. While you're at it, stop by your stupid ass parents' house and give this to your shiesty ass daddy. While you're at it, tell them motherfuckers that raised you if they even think about touching or seeing my son again, I'll kill their ass."

Yah-Yah threw a big ass duffle bag on the bed and proceeded to throw the other bed lamp at my ass. That time it nicked my ear. I could feel the blood trickling down the side of my neck, but I was more concerned about the tears flowing down her face.

"Shhh! Stop crying! I'm sorry." She was trying her best to get out of my hands, but I was holding onto her as tight as I could. It warmed a nigga's heart to finally see her tough as shedding tears.

"Let me gooooo!"

"No! I'm not letting you go. Just stop crying first."

"I can't believe you were going to marry her and leave us. I hate you."

"Stop it with the damn dramatics Ka'Jaiyah! I would never leave you and my son. Your ass knows all I've tried to do was show you that I love, but you be fighting that shit with your behavior. I would have been pulled this shit had I known all it took was for me to fuck with another bitch in order to get you to behave. Now wipe your damn face and get dressed. We need to go and talk to your father."

I let her go and started getting dressed we were wasting valuable time dealing with this shit she was doing.

"Talk to him for what?'"

"I know you killed Raja, and because you did that, we're about to be in war. Don' t ask any questions or look for explanations. Just know that I know why you did it. I need you to know that I love you more than anything in this world. I chose you when my father told me to choose between you and being head of the family. I don't regret that decision, so I need you to prove them wrong. They say you aren't worthy of having my heart or my son. I say you're worthy of it all and more. Raja was business. This thing with you is very personal, my love. Now get dressed. We got shit to do." I smacked her on the ass as she walked into the bathroom.

After I was completely dressed, I sat on the side of the bed and flamed up another blunt. Staring at all of the money that had fallen out of the duffle bag and onto the floor had me in my feelings. It was hard for me to understand why he was going to such great lengths to keep us apart. The wheels in my head were turning, and I realized since all of this shit had kicked off Yasir had become distant. My mother was on my father's side no matter what. It's fucked up that I can't even trust my own family and that's fucking me up.

"I'm ready."

Looking up at Yah-Yah standing over me made my dick get hard again. She was now dressed in a Champion jogging suit and rocking some Air Max 95. I placed my fitted cap on my head and grabbed her hand so that we could head out.

During the ride, Yah-Yah was holding my hand tight as hell. I had to remove my shit from her grip to get some damn circulation. We were in silence as we sipped on some Rémy and passed a blunt back and forth between us. It was pouring down raining, so it was taking longer to get to her parents' crib with them living out in the damn boondocks.

"I was never going to take that money, Yahmeen. No amount of money could replace you."

"I'm happy to know that. I'm sorry for what he did. He should never have come at you like that. Just so we're clear my parents will never get our son. I need you to promise me that you're going to follow my lead and hop in when I need you. Your ass is a loose cannon, and it scares me. Tonight I watched you warp into a boss ass bitch. The way you handled Raja made my dick hard."

"Wait a minute. You were in there?"

"You might as well say I was. I had cameras placed inside her apartment the moment she thought it was a good idea for us to get married. All along the bitch had her an agenda and wanted to be head of the shit her father was running. Once I got what I needed, I was going to murk her ass anyway!"

"I should fuck you up, Yahmeen!"

"For what?"

"You put me through all of that bullshit, and none of it was real. Why you just couldn't tell me instead of just doing it this way.

"For one I had to teach your ass a lesson, and for two, you should know me better than to marry a bitch out of the blue like that."

I was getting ready to say something else, but a mirage of bullets came out of nowhere. The last thing I heard was Yah-Yah screaming before we smashed head-on into a tree.

Chapter Twelve

YAH-YAH

The sound of my father breaking shit and going crazy woke me up from my sleep. He had been going ape shit since the accident. As for me, I was trying to keep calm. One thing for sure and two things for certain I know that Yahmeen didn't leave me to die. That's what it looks like, but nothing will make me believe it. Apparently, when the police arrived at the accident scene, I was in the passenger seat unconscious, and Yahmeen was gone. Something wasn't right and just hearing my daddy cussing let me know that I needed to let him know what was going on. That added with my brothers terrorizing the city and burning down all Yahmeen spots. With all of this going on, my father still hasn't spoken a word to me. Like he came to the hospital to make sure I was cool but said nothing to me. My emotions were all over the place, and I needed a release.

Despite the car being shot up and hitting a tree, all I had was a concussion and bruises. Looking at pictures of the car, it was a wonder I survived. As I looked over at my sleeping son, tears welled up in my eyes. Just the thought of not knowing where Yahmeen is at is killing me. He would never not check on our son. Something is seriously wrong, and I can feel it in my heart. Grabbing my phone, I called and texted his phone for the millionth time. I threw my phone up against the wall, and it shattered into pieces. I was so frustrated and angry that I didn't know what to do.

"What the hell is going on in here?" my momma said as she rushed inside of my old bedroom.

"Ma, something is wrong with Yahmeen!" I cried.

"Wipe your motherfucking face! That chump ass nigga left you like you was a side bitch or something. He better hope your daddy and brothers make it to his ass first because If I get a hold to his bitch ass, I'm going to torture his ass and feed him to the lions at Brookfield Zoo.

"No ma! You don't understand. Before the accident, we made up. It's something I need to tell you and daddy, but I know you're going to be mad!"

"Mad about what!" My father was now standing in the doorway looking pissed and very intoxicated. He had this wild look in his eyes. I hadn't seen that look in years, but I know it meant he was ready for war.

"Don't get quiet now, Ka'Jaiyah! You heard your father. What the fuck are we going to be mad about? I doubt the bullshit trumps the fact that the nigga we gave permission to marry you abandoned your ass when you needed him the most!"

My mother was yelling so loud she woke up my baby. Before I could grab him, she grabbed him first. The way they were both staring at me let me know that wanted me to start talking.

"Before I start talking, can curse daddy?"

"Yes! You can curse, Yah-Yah!"

"Okay, so the day before the accident Yahmeen's father came to the house and offered me money to never speak to him. Basically, he didn't want me to be with his son and told me that I was standing in the way of him marrying the bitch Raja! That shit was basically for business. That man doesn't love Yahmeen. He's nothing but a cash cow. They were making him marry that bitch for money purposes. He was so damn disrespectful to me! I lost it when he told me that I needed to turn over my parental rights to Jr. because I was unfit. Before I knew it, I upped my gun on his ass and told him to get the fuck out of my shit. I made sure to take the money though. I needed to show that shit to Yahmeen so that he could know how the fuck his people really feel about him.

I was so mad and in my feelings after that so I went to his bitch's condo! That same money his father offered me, I offered that hoe to leave Yahmeen alone! I would never allow that man to live in peace with another woman. Ain't no motherfucking breaking up! She got smart, so I killed her ass. I hit that hoe right between the eyes for popping slick! Unbeknownst to me, Yahmeen had cameras in her house because he didn't trust her. Come to find out that bitch had her own agenda against him while he had his own agenda against her. That whole wedding was for them to be the heads of their family businesses.

Before the accident, Yahmeen came to me and came clean about everything. I know for a fact that man didn't leave me for dead! I'm telling y'all something is wrong. Somebody got him, daddyyyy!" I couldn't help myself at this point. All I could do was cry my eyes out because something was wrong.

"Why the fuck you ain't been said this shit, Yah-Yah?"

"Because daddyyy! You haven't been talking to me behind my behavior. This was something that I wanted to deal with on my own. I needed to show you that I could handle things the grown-up way. It hurt me that you wouldn't talk to me, so the last thing I wanted to do was bother you or ma. I'm sorry I didn't control my anger and killed that bitch, but she asked for it. Yahmeen loves me, and I know something is not right. I don't trust his father. That man is a snake, and he makes my skin crawl. I never want him or Yahmeen's mother around my son again.

"You don't even have to worry about that! My grandson is not going around either of them snake ass bitches. I knew it was a reason I didn't like that hoe. Let me call the Boss Ladies. It's time for us to regulate around this bitch!"

"I thought y'all were retired?"

"Fuck retirement when it comes down to my husband and my children! I'll kill a brick and a building for my family. If you're feeling up to it, get dressed. We got shit to do.

"Nah! She's going with me today! Yah-Yah needs the Thug Inc.

experience. I mean we taught them Boss Ladies everything they know."

My momma rolled her eyes and stuck her finger up before walking out of the door. My heart warmed a little at the thought of my father wanting me to be with him.

"I'm sorry for disappointing you, daddy." I wiped the tears from my eyes as my father came and sat on the bed next to me.

"Stop crying. I accept your apology, but I have to apologize to you as well. I've always given you a life that allowed you to think certain shit was okay. I've never given you boundaries. That was my first mistake with you. All of your life I've allowed you to do whatever the fuck you wanted, and that hurt your relationship as a future wife. However, I'm proud of you because you handled this situation well. Who taught you how to shoot?"

"Really, daddy! You taught me how to shoot."

"Nah! What did I really teach you?"

"Shoot first and fuck questions! I'm a Kenneth. Whatever I say it is that's what the fuck it is!"

"That a girl. I would never apologize for treating you the way I have. That shit was needed in order for you to understand where the fuck I was coming from. Are you sure that nigga wouldn't leave you because I got money on his head? I need to know if you have that much faith in that nigga because I want him dead or alive.

"Yahmeen would never abandon me behind what happened. If I cut up, then he got at me in his own way. Daddy, I'm hardcore, but that man loves me. It took for him to literally leave me to show me that I'm in love with him. To the world, I'm the daughter of a thug, but all I want is to be the wife of a gangsta. Yahmeen don't play, daddy. I'm telling you something is wrong. He would never play about me and our son. He was happy that I murked Raja. That's how I know something is not right. Whoever shot that car up has Yahmeen! Please, daddy, don't kill him because I know this is not his doing." I was literally in tears.

My father grabbed me and held me tight. For the first times in months, I felt so loved in the arms of my father. To the world, he was the infamous Thug, the man the streets feared, and the man women loved. In that moment, he was simply the man who gave me life and showed me how to protect myself from the cruelties of the world. My mother would die if she knew my father had been grooming me to kill shit since I was seven years old.

"I'll call the hit off, but if I find out that nigga's a snake, I want his head! Let me call your brothers and stop them. They've been on a rampage."

I looked at my father through narrowed eyes because there was no telling what he had them out there doing.

"Oh my god! Let me hurry up and get dressed to find them."

"Nah! You stay here and keep resting. I don't need you out in them streets right now. Let me and your brothers handle this shit. Plus, concussions are serious so just chill, Yah-Yah. By the way, I'm proud of the way you handled yourself. No matter what, don't ever let a nigga or a bitch disrespect you. If a motherfucker forgets who the fuck you are, always remind their ass. Don't take any bullshit period. Now, don't think I'm telling you to be out here wilding. I just want you to do shit the right way. You just caught your first body, and I'm positive you'll be catching more. " My father kissed me on the forehead and walked out of the room.

For the most part, I was happy that I was able to get everything off my chest. Not telling my parents about what happened was weighing heavy on me. Being back on good terms with my father means everything to me. The look in his eyes let me know that he was absolutely proud of me for the way that I handled myself. I know that my mother is too.

For a couple of minutes my mind had stopped worrying about Yahmeen, but the moment I looked at my son, I teared up. Grabbing my phone, I started calling him like crazy with no such luck. This shit was hurting me to the point where my head started hurting. As I sat thinking about where Yahmeen could be, I became angry. In that moment, I was feeling like I wasn't doing enough. My nigga could be somewhere in the gutter bleeding, and I'm in the damn bed nursing a concussion. Jumping out of bed, I went in search of my younger siblings. I found Kaia, Kahari, and Kylie all in the game room playing *Fortnite*.

"I need to make a run somewhere real quick. Can y'all keep an eye on Jr. for me?"

"Daddy said to call him if you got out of the bed," Kaia spoke up without looking at me. I rolled my eyes because her ass was a tattletale.

"I'll give each of you one hundred dollars to do this for me."

"You got yourself a deal," Kahari added without even looking up from the game. His ass lived and breathed *Fortnite*. Kylie didn't care either way. She's the sweetest kid I know.

"Don't go getting in trouble, Yah-Yah. You know daddy's gone snap if you do."

"I know Kylie, and I promise that I won't."

"Yeah right!" Kaia said as she laughed.

I ignored her little ass, and I quickly got dressed. While getting dressed to leave, I realized my car was still at my house. Thinking on my feet, I realized that I had to take one of my parents' cars. I chose my momma's Benz truck because she was more lenient with us kids driving her shit. Not my Daddy though. He'll buy you whatever kind of car you want, but driving his shit is out of the question.

Hopping inside the car, I made sure to check the secret compartments she kept her guns in. My momma was like a nigga. That woman kept guns on deck. After making sure that I was locked and loaded, I headed directly to Yahmeen's parent's house. They had to know where he was at. There is no way in hell they didn't. It bothered me that Yasir hadn't reached out either. At one point he was so far up Heaven's ass that he could smell her shit. Now all of a sudden, she hasn't heard from his ass. I really don't know what the fuck is going on, but one thing for sure and two for certain I'm about to get down to the bottom of this shit.

§

About an hour later, I was pulling up to their estate but stopped when I saw all of the police cars and yellow tape that blocked everything off. The shit looked just like the movie *Belly* when they took Ox's ass out. The shit had me fearing the worse, and I just started crying hysterically. At first, I wanted just to drive off, but I couldn't. I needed to see what the fuck was going out. I hauled ass trying to make it up the driveway. As soon as I saw Yasir trying to get past the police, my heart sank.

"Yasirrrrr! Where is Yahmeen? Pleaseeeee, tell me that he's okay." I was grabbing his ass all in his collar. I didn't give a fuck that he had tears streaming down his face.

"Please step back! This is a homicide investigation," a police officer said, which made more officers come over and make both of us move.

"What the fuck is he talking about homicide investigation? Please, Yasir, tell me what the fuck is going on?" I was about ten minutes away from slapping the shit out of him. He was pissing me off crying and acting like he was mute.

"Somebody killed my mother and father! I came home and found them dead! I swear to God I'm going to find out who the fuck did this shit and bury their asses.

"Where is Yahmeen?" I angrily asked because if their parents were dead then where in the hell was my nigga.

"I don't know, Yah-Yah. That's actually why I came over here to holla at my pops. To my understanding, Raja's father was blaming Yahmeen for her murder, and they were the ones who shot the car up. My father got word as to what was about to go down, and he managed to find the car flipped over. From what my momma told me, they put Yahmeen up where Raja's people couldn't find him. That added with the fact that he is in a coma somewhere. The accident fucked him up. My mother was so damn afraid of my father that she wouldn't tell me anything more out of fear that he would get her. Only my father knows where Yahmeen is, and at this point, it's looking like we'll never know if he's alive or dead."

Yasir was now crying uncontrollably, and me on the other hand, I was numb. I felt nothing because, in all actuality, I didn't know how to feel. In my heart, I know that there is so much more to this shit. At the same time, I feel like Yahmeen's father is behind all of this shit. A part of me hopes that he's not really dead so that I can find out where the fuck Yahmeen is. I'm not going to believe or put it out in the atmosphere that he's dead. The love I have for that man would never allow me to give up on him like that.

Thoughts of my son consumed me as I somberly headed back to my parents' house. I had spent so much time bullshitting and taking my relationship for granted, and now it seems like I'll never get Yahmeen back. This shit is not fair at all. I'm not even thinking about my stupid ass and my antics. I'm more worried about my son and how he's so young that he doesn't understand what the hell is going on around him. This shit was hurting my soul. Our future had been cut short by the demons of our present. I would give anything to be able to go back and change the events that led to this. I'm responsible because had I not killed that girl, Yahmeen would be cool. The way I feel now, I would rather see him married to someone else than not be here to raise our son. I guess it's true when they say love people when you can because you never know when they won't be here anymore.

Chapter Thirteen

HEAVEN

Six Months Later

It had been six months since Yahmeen disappeared and the shit was hard as hell on Yah-Yah. My girl was so brokenhearted that she couldn't even function. Long gone was feisty, smart mouth ass Yah-Yah. Yahmeen's disappearance had my girl sick. Being six months pregnant didn't help either. From what she says the night before the accident that had the best lovemaking session in the world. She feels like Yahmeen got her pregnant on purpose because he knew what the fuck was up. I was trying my best to be a good friend and cousin to Yah-Yah, but it was hard watching her cry all day every day.

Besides Yah-Yah being fucked up, Yasir was too. He and I were now in a relationship, and I'm the happiest I've been in a long time. Lil Dro is sick as fuck, and I could care less. He had a good girl in me and lost me. After the way he handled me, there was no coming back from that shit. He called himself trying to get one over on the bitch he was fucking with because he believed the baby wasn't his, but it was. Now he has to deal with her nutty ass and that baby because I want no parts of his stupid ass.

At first, I thought that Lil Dro was going to be on bullshit with Yasir and I being together, but my daddy nipped that shit in the bud quick. Lil Dro knows Remy Ramirez don't play period. I used to be so hurt watching him love on that bitch because that's all I wanted from him. Now, I laugh because he looks miserable as hell. I'm just happy he does right by Heaven. I've even started allowing her to go and be with him again. I refuse to be a bitter ass baby momma. These hoes be walking around mad because a nigga fucked them over, so they use their children as a pawn. I'm not cut like them type of bitches. Heaven loves her daddy, and as long as I have breath in my body, I'll never speak a bad word on his name in front of her. My daughter will not be one of those kids that grow up and think it's okay to disrespect her father because of our personal issues. Any way that I feel about his stupid ass I'll speak on when she's not present.

Being with Yasir has been everything and more. We've recently moved in together, and he loves Heaven as if she was his own. Lil Dro hates that shit too, but after his parents had a good talk with his ass, he piped down. I'm just glad Yasir never let them punk him. Without Yahmeen even being around, my baby can hold his own, and that's what I love the most about him. You have got to be a tough mother-fucker to deal with Legacy Inc. Outside of Lil Dro being the father of my child, my cousins ran shit. They would beat a nigga ass behind the girls in the family.

Hell, once Yasir won my father over, I knew he was something special or slicker than a bitch. My ass had been trying to find anything wrong with him, but he never showed me a flaw that made want to run far away from his ass. Lil Dro hurt me to the core, so I was cautious with giving my heart again. I couldn't punish Yasir for the shit that Dro had done to me. He didn't deserve that because he had been here for me when I needed him the most. After trying my best to give him the run around about being together, I finally gave in. I'm so happy because it's the best decision that I've ever made.

§

"Come on, Yah-Yah. We have got to pick out a theme for the baby shower." She was laying her ass on the couch eating a big ass bag of Flaming Hot Doritos. It had been well over an hour, and she didn't seem the least bit interested in her baby shower. Her momma didn't have any luck persuading her, so she thought I would be of better help. From the looks of it, I can't get her to get into this shit either.

"I'm going to tell you like I told my momma. I don't want a baby shower. Hell, I don't even want this baby. Please leave me alone, Heaven."

"I know that you're hurting behind not knowing where Yahmeen is, but don't say that about the baby."

"Do you really know that I'm hurting, Heaven? I doubt that you do because if you did you wouldn't be pressuring me to have a damn baby shower. What type of baby shower will it be? How can I actually enjoy it with Yahmeen not being present? It seems like I'm the only mother-fucker who gets that he's not here. Everybody is walking around all happy and in love while my nigga is missing. Just leave, Heaven, I'm sure Yasir is somewhere planning y'all another vacation or putting in an order for you some roses. Why the fuck are you over here anyway?"

I would be ready to go off had this been any other time. However, because I know she's in a bad place, I'm going to let her slide. At the same time, I'm about to grab my shit and leave. Although I understand that she's grieving, I haven't matured to that place where I'm going to allow someone to keep talking shit to me, and I don't clap back.

"You're right, Yah-Yah. I don't know how it feels, but I know you. That shit you just said about that baby is not you speaking. You love that unborn baby and Jr. Do you actually think that Yahmeen would want you to be sitting around like this? That man loved you with everything inside of him. The least you could do is love his seeds enough for the both of you. Now keep laying your fat ass up there in them Doritos you gone be big as a fucking house. In the meantime, bitch, I'm going to put this baby shower together, and you will be there with bells on. Do not fuck with me Ka'Jaiyah!"

I grabbed my damn Chanel bag, placed on my matching shades, and left her ass there on the couch looking crazy. I've spent six months dealing with her shit, and I'm no longer pacifying her ass. It's time she embraces what the fuck is really going on. I don't have time for this bratty shit with her.

About thirty minutes later, I was walking into the condo that I shared with Yasir. He was talking on the phone, and when he noticed that I had come inside the room, he quickly hung up. I took notice of that because he had done that a couple of times this past week. Of course, my senses heightened, but I decided to keep them under wraps. He had been handling his family's affairs, so he could have very well been on the phone with an associate. The last thing I wanted to look like was an insecure female.

"Hey, babe! I missed you so much today." I jumped into his arms and wrapped my arms around his neck. His Givenchy cologne smelled so good as it invaded my nostrils. It was the type of scent that made a bitch panties wet.

"Is that right?" he said as he lifted me from my feet and carried me over to the couch. Laying me down, he wasted no time dropping to his knees and forcefully pulling my legs apart. He smacked my bare pussy with his hand, and that shit made me wet.

"'Fuck your panties at? You know I hate it when you don't rock underwear and shit."

"I know, but I didn't like how they looked in my dress," I whined at the same time biting my lip as he dived in my pussy had first.

I couldn't do shit but wrap my legs around his head. The feeling of his tongue flicking back forth against my clit was sending sensual waves throughout my entire body. Yasir ate my pussy like a champ. I see why all his hoes have been hating on my pretty ass.

"I'm about to cummmmm!" I moaned out as I grabbed his head and pushed his face deeper into my pussy. He was saying something, but I couldn't hear him because his mouth was full. As I squirted, the sound of his phone vibrating irritated me. Whoever the fuck it was needed to wait. I could tell he was getting ready to reach for it, but I stopped his ass. He stood up, but I grabbed him.

"That might be one of my workers."

"Fuck them workers."

I pushed him down on the couch and straddled him. I kissed him passionately as he lifted me just enough so that I could sit on his dick. I planted my feet flat so that I could have all access to his massive dick. I loved how Dro would make love to me, but the shit Yasir does to my body is out of this world. I fell forward and sucked on his neck as he roughly pounded in and out of me. He grabbed my ponytail and pulled my back so that he could kiss me. I could feel his juices running down my legs as I lifted up off him. He wasted no time getting up and grabbing his phone. I rolled my eyes and headed up to the bedroom to take a shower.

"Why the fuck you walk off like that?"

"I just wanted to give you some privacy. It's obvious that's what you need." He started laughing and stared at him through narrow eyes because I didn't see shit funny. He pulled me into his embrace and stared at into my eyes.

"I know you've been through some shit and I'm not trying to add to it. All I want to do is love you and make you happy. I promise you have nothing to worry about."

"I'm not worried about shit."

"You ain't worried, but your ass is pouting like a big baby." I couldn't help but laugh because he was right.

"I love you, Yasir."

"I love you more. Now get dressed I want to take you out to dinner." He smacked me on my ass and walked off.

As I took I shower, I realized just how much of a brave front Yasir had been putting on in the midst of Yahmeen's absence. In my opinion, he's almost too calm for his only brother and best friend to be missing and most likely dead. Looking up to see Yasir stepping inside of the shower broke me from my thoughts, and I focused on his massive hard-on. He wasted no time turning me around and going balls deep inside of me. All my thoughts left my mind and were replaced with pure ecstasy. Yasir always fucked me as if he was trying to prove a point. He had that type of lovemaking that makes a bitch go looking for his ass with a flashlight. I seriously felt this nigga was gone have me fucking some shit up behind fucking me like this. I don't know what it was.

Lil Dro was my first love, and I was so in love with him. I really thought it didn't get any better besides him. With Yasir shit is different though it's like he's showing me what's it's like to be loved by a man with no limitations. He's so soft and gentle with me, not to mention he's so caring and loving. He's like a dream come true, and he came at the time that I needed him the most. I pray this shit never changes because I want to love on him forever.

♨

"Thank you for taking us out to dinner."

"Stop thanking me, Heaven. I'm your nigga, and that's what I'm supposed to do." He leaned over and stroked Remy Ma's cheek, and she giggled like crazy. I just stared out him and loved how he doted on both my daughter and me.

"It must feel good trying to be me, nigga."

The sound of Dro's voice irritated the fuck out of me. Out of all the fucking restaurants to be at, this nigga would be the same Long-horn Steakhouse we were at. He had this crazy wild look in his eyes, and I knew it was about to be some shit. I was so damn tired of his shenanigans. It was always some bullshit when I picked our daughter up or dropped her off with his ass.

"Don't nobody want to be you, nigga! I'm simply taking my woman and her daughter on a dinner date. I thought we discussed this, nigga! Are you still in your feelings about me being with Heaven?

"Nigga, I don't have no feelings! I don't give a fuck about what the fuck you do with Heaven, but this beauty right here came from my nut sack! Stop walking around here trying to be stepdaddy of the year. My daughter only got one motherfucking daddy. When your stupid ass gets through entertaining, she'll be at my crib, and you can come get her! I already told your stupid looking ass to stop trying to build a family with my fucking daughter!"

"Nigga, watch your motherfucking mouth talking to her like that!" Yasir had jumped up to fight Lil Dro, and he was laughing as if some shit was funny.

"You better sit your chump ass down! Don't let the love you have for Heaven get you murked! You think your brother's missing! Your ass will be missing right with his ass. Don't fuck with me bitch ass nigga!" Before I knew it, Yasir swung and knocked the fuck out of Lil Dro. From the point on it was pandemonium, and the entire restaurant was screaming and scattering.

"Stop it! Y'all are scaring my babyyy!" I was crying because Remy Ma was screaming and hollering at the top of her lungs.

"Shut the fuck up and move!"

Lil Dro pushed me so hard that I fell back on my ass. Yasir morphed and started beating Lil Dro's ass. That shit only made Lil Dro angrier and started fighting Yasir like a damn animal. Both of these niggas was tearing this fucking restaurant up. The moment that I saw Lil Dro's stupid ass pull his gun out, I grabbed my daughter and got the fuck out of there. Instead of going home, I went to Ms. Khia's house. She needed to talk to Dro before I told my daddy on his ignorant ass. I'm sick of trying to hold shit back to keep the peace. Dro was doing too much.

My phone was ringing like crazy, and I didn't give a fuck who it was. I was pissed at Yasir for feeding into Lil Dro's bullshit. I'm with him, so there is never a need for him to feel like he has to fight Lil Dro. That man wanted to ruin our dinner, and Yasir helped him do it. I'm pissed off at both of their stupid asses. They're supposed to both love Remy Ma, but they're fighting and acting a damn fool in front her. They had better hope my daddy don't find out about this bullshit.

❦

"I've told Lil Dro to stop walking around here doing stupid shit! He made his bed, so he needs to lie down in it. His sneaky dick ass was over there fucking with that hood rat ass bitch, and you moved on. He's been acting a damn fool in the streets too. That motherfucker burnt down all Yasir blocks."

My eyes bulged out of my head because that was news to me. Yasir never said anything about it to me.

"That lil nigga gone make me fuck him up! I'm telling you, Khia. You better talk to his ass. He's supposed to know that fighting in front of his daughter is not cool. All this shit he out here doing in them streets is not good for business. I'm fed the fuck up with that lil nigga and his bullshit."

No sooner than the words left his father's mouth, Lil Dro walked his crazy ass through the door. The fact that he had a damn fifth of

Rémy drinking from the bottle made me shake my head at his dumb ass. I don't know who this nigga was, but he was a complete fucking turn off. I can't believe I used to let this clown make me cry.

"Next time you go out on a date with that bitch ass nigga, drop my daughter off!" He rushed me and basically cornered me in the kitchen.

"Khiandre get the fuck outta my face! I don't say shit to you when you have my baby around that damn boogabear you got for a baby momma. What the fuck is wrong with you? You know that I'm with Yasir now just like I know you with that hoe. I'm not understanding where all of this anger is coming from. "

"You belong to me, Heaven!" he yelled in my face causing me to jump back. I was glad his parents were still in the kitchen with us.

"But you belong to somebody else!"

"I don't want that bitch. I want you and my daughter! Fuck that nigga! You might as well get comfortable because your ass is not going anywhere! Hey, my Remmyyyy Ma! You love dadddy, don't you! Fuck that nigga Yasir!" He was now staggering and all in my baby face kissing on her.

"I'm about to go home, and I suggest you do the same, Khiandre!"

"What the fuck I say, Heaven?"

"You better not even think about putting your hands on that girl. What the fuck is up with you, son? This ain't the man I raised you to be. Let Heaven and Remy Ma go home. We need to talk, and you need to sleep that shit off, not to mention take your ass to the hospital. Your knuckles are all fucked up and shit."

"That's what happens when you beat a fuck nigga ass! Now, like I said, get comfortable because you or my daughter not leaving this house." Lil Dro grabbed me by my face and squeezed it as tight as he could. I reached back and slapped the fuck out of him. I was officially fed up with his fuck shit. After that slap, Khia followed up and slapped the fuck out of him.

"I swear to God I tried to raise you to be better than that crazy bitch Nico. As I stand here looking at you, all I can see is his horrible ass, the same nigga in the flesh that liked to verbally and physically abuse women."

"What the fuck you thought was going to happen? Pops raised me and gave me a life, but the fact remains the same that infamous nigga Nico is my father. They say that crazy shit is hereditary! I didn't believe it until I went to talk to someone about these fucking blackouts and violent rages I've been having. So, yes, I am just like him. Don't blame me for my behavior. You should have thought about that before you fucked your best friend's nigga!"

"I'm about to beat this nigga's ass!" Big Dro walked full speed towards Lil Dro, but Khia stopped him.

"No! He's right. This is all my fault." Khia now had tears streaming down her face. I knew this would hurt him. I fucked up, babe!"

Big Dro was now trying to console her, and if I didn't hate his ass before, I definitely hate his ass now. I had a baby with a damn stranger.

"Khiandre, how could you talk to her like that?"

I grabbed my daughter and pushed right past his dumb ass. His behavior was out of control and uncalled for. I knew the backstory on Khia and Aunt Tahari in regards to Khiandre's birth father, Nico. She was a good mother to him, and she didn't deserve the shit he said to her. As I strapped my daughter in the car seat, I stared at her. All I could do was pray that she didn't inherit that crazy ass shit. I would lose my fucking mind if she did.

Heading towards my house, it started to rain, and all I could think about was Yasir. I was feeling real fucked up. There I was dealing with Lil Dro drama, and I should have been checking on Yasir. That man was literally fighting and fucking my baby daddy up behind me. For a quick second, I wondered if I still loved Lil Dro. I quickly shook that thought from my mind. I know for a fact I love Yasir.

Heading towards our house, I tried calling him, but he never answered. As a matter of fact, his phone was now going straight to voicemail. My heartbeat started to race out of fear that something had gone terribly wrong. I was regretting ever going out to dinner at this point. One minute everything was cool and the next everything was fucked up.

Chapter Fourteen

YASIR

Heaven had me so fucked up! There I was standing in the middle of a fucking restaurant defending her honor, and she dips out on my ass. The fact that she didn't even stay to make sure that I was straight got me heated. At the same time, I hated the fact that the shit made her and the baby scared. There wasn't an ounce of hoe in my blood, so I was with whatever time that nigga was on with it.

Yes, I'll defend my girl no matter what, but this shit is bigger than Heaven. It's about me as a man. I would never let him, or any nigga in this world think they can punk me! My name might not hold as much weight as them Legacy Inc. niggas do in the street, but at the end of the day, I'm still out here holding shit down on my own. That bitch ass nigga Lil Dro don't have to like me, but he will respect me. With my father being dead and not knowing where my brother is, I have a lot on my fucking plate. I'll fuck around and kill me a motherfucker. That's why I'm packing my shit and getting the fuck out of here before I hurt Heaven.

My goal was to leave before she made it in the house. I wasn't dipping on her like a fuck nigga. I just need my space. Hearing the security system let me know that Heaven had made it home, much to my dismay. I quickly grabbed what I had packed and headed down the stairs.

"Oh my god! Look at your face! Babe, it looks like your nose is broken."

She stood in front of me and reached out to touch my nose, but I knocked her hand away. I was already in pain and pissed off because I had let that nigga get a good ass hit in.

"Move, Heaven!"

"What you mean move? Where are you going, Yasir?" I tried walking around her, but she would block my path.

"Look, Heaven, right now I need to get some air away from you." It hurt me to say that, but it was the truth. I know for a fact Heaven loves me, but I can't help but think about if she still loves that nigga.

"Why do you need air from me? What did I do?" Her voice creaked, and her eyes were glossy. I felt fucked up about making her cry because that's the last thing I want to do to.

"Tonight when that shit went down where did you go? There is no way I should have beat you here, not to mention you didn't answer the phone, and I called you repeatedly until my fucking phone died! Please don't lie because I don't lie to you about shit."

I watched her bite her lips and think about what the hell she was going to say.

"I went to Dro's parents' house so that they could talk to him about all of this crazy shit he's doing."

"At any moment did you think about me and if I was okay. At the end of the day, I could have been somewhere dead, and you wouldn't give a fuck. Last time I checked, you and I were in a relationship. You still love that nigga or something?"

"What! No, Yasir. I love you. At the end of the day, I only went over there so they could stop his bullshit. I'm sorry for going over there and not coming home, but you have no idea how hard it is to see y'all fighting like that. My baby was screaming and crying and neither one of y'all stopped. "

Heaven was crying and hysterical at this point. I just grabbed and hugged her tight as I could.

"I just need some air. With everything that's going on in my life, this shit is weighing down on me. I love you Heaven, but I need to make sure that with me is where you want to be.

"Bye Yasir! If you want to leave then leave, I don't give a fuck. I'm damned if I do and damned if I don't. Finally, I let you love me, and this is what you do. You better hope I still want your black ass after you get some air!"

She stepped to the side and let me pass, which I was glad she did because I didn't want to physically move her ass. Before walking out of the door, I made sure to kiss Remy Ma before walking out. I loved her and Heaven with everything inside of me, but before proceeding, I need Heaven to prove she's for me and me only.

Once I got inside the car, my emotions got the best of me. I just started beating the steering wheel over and over again. Reality really set in that my fucking parents were gone, and I had no clue where my brother was at. In my heart, I felt like he was cool. On the other hand, my father was a tyrant, and when you defied him, he made you pay. Leaning back on the headrest I realized that all I had was Heaven. I have more money and houses than I know what to do with, but it means nothing if I have to be there alone. I can be with any bitch I want, but I want Heaven. I've always wanted Heaven.

Putting my pride to the side, I hopped out the car and went back in the house. Heaven was balled up on the couch crying hard as fuck, and that shit hurt me. Remy Ma was lying on top of her not understanding what was wrong.

"Look, man, stop crying. I'm not leaving, and I should never have said that shit to you in the first place.

"I don't love him anymore. I love you, Yasir," she cried so hard, and all I could do was sit beside her.

"Momma sad!"

"Come on now, Heaven. Stop crying like this. Remy Ma is scared. She's been through enough tonight."

I needed to do something to distract Remy Ma so that I could calm Heaven down. She loved *Moana,* so I put the TV on for her to watch. That would hold her attention until it went off. As I grabbed her a juice and some Cheetos, I noticed Heaven head upstairs. Once I made sure she was situated I headed up the stairs to find Heaven. Walking into our bedroom, I could hear the shower running. At first, I wanted to give her some space but fuck all that. She needed to know that I fucked with her. I just didn't like how she didn't check on me.

I got undressed and joined her in the shower. As soon as the water hit my damn face that shit hurt. I was almost certain my nose was fucked up. That shit made me mad as fuck, and I wanted to fight that nigga some more.

"Stop crying, okay. We good. Let's just fuck and make up."

Heaven didn't respond, but her body did. The sight of her nipples perking up made a nigga want to latch on to them shits like a baby getting breastfed. I pinned her against the wall, and as I lifted her, I wrapped her legs around my waist. Without hesitation, I rammed my dick inside of her. She needed to feel all of this pressure."

"Ahhh!"

As I roughly pumped in and out of her, the alarm started to go off like crazy. I quickly jumped out of the shower bussing my shit in the process. Heaven was right behind me slipping and sliding. We were both naked as the day we born trying to run down the stairs to see what the fuck was going. My heart stopped seeing that Remy Ma was no longer on the couch and the front door was wide open.

"Where's my baby at!" Heaven was panicking walking all over the house looking for her, but some shit told me that nigga Lil Dro was behind this shit. I immediately rushed to the security panel and rolled the tape back. Just as I thought, his ass had kidnapped his own damn daughter. I was kicking my own ass for leaving her downstairs alone.

"Calm down. That bitch ass nigga got her!" Heaven rushed over to where I was and watched the footage.

"That's it. I'm calling my daddy. This nigga has fucked with me for the last time."

I was trying my best not to murk this nigga. It looked like that's what I was going to have to do in order to bring some peace to Heaven. What type of nigga would I be if I allowed her ex to cross our threshold and get away with it? Game the fuck over!

Chapter Fifteen

YAH-YAH

Despite the current depression I was going through, I needed to cheer up Heaven. Lil Dro had taken the damn baby and was gone on vacation. Nobody knew where he was, and Remy was livid. This nigga had so much friction going on within the family that it made no sense. I knew for a fact my brothers knew where his dumb ass was. They just were acting dumb. We all knew he wouldn't hurt Remy Ma, but the fact remains the same— he took her from her mother.

Heaven walking around here losing weight like a bitch suffering from anorexia, and it's only been a week. At the same time, I understand how when shit happens it makes you not want to live anymore. The only reason why I haven't checked myself into a mental hospital is because my son needs me, not to mention my family has been so supportive despite me being a bitch to everybody. I just knew my baby was going to either come out a crybaby or mean as fuck. I had been both since the moment that I found out I was pregnant.

It's now been seven months since Yahmeen disappeared, and I'm still waking up with a tear-stained pillow. Nothing about his absence has gotten easier. I guess that's because I have no idea where the fuck he is. The way I feel, I would rather know that he's actually dead. At least I would have a grave or ashes to talk to. Sometimes I feel like Yasir knows something and isn't telling me. I swear I'm going to kill him if he's keeping anything from me. It's crazy how everybody in his family is dead or missing, but he's here untouched, not to mention running the family business. Yeah, some shit was not sitting right with me, but I would keep my thoughts to myself.

My daddy already thought I was driving myself crazy mourning. I hate to feel like there is a conspiracy going on, but shit just don't feel right. I had been so deep in thought that I forgot Heaven and I were sitting at her house chilling in her bed. For the last two days, I've been staying with her just to keep her since Yasir had to go out of town for a business meeting.

"He still didn't answer?"

"No, but he posting on IG like shit was cool. Look at this bitch. Why is he doing this? I just want my baby back home. His stupid ass has cut off the comments."

Heaven handed me her phone, and Lil Dro was chilling on a beach with Remy Ma surrounded by beautiful blue water. His caption read *Chilling with my forever girl! Don't trip! Be cool! Daddy's baby is straight.*

"Uncle Remy gone beat that boy's ass when he comes back." I couldn't do shit but laugh because Lil Dro thought this shit was a game.

"I'm so mad at him for all this drama he's started. My daddy wants to kill him, and my momma talking about beating Khia up on sight."

"Wait a minute. Why does she want to fight Khia?"

"She swears that lady is hiding him out. No matter how much I try to convince her that she's worried and distraught too, my momma is not trying to hear it. Khia is really hurt behind this shit, and she feels responsible. I'm telling you she ain't been right since that nigga blamed her for fucking that nigga. I was hurt for her."

"Yeah, I overheard her and my momma talking. That nigga Nico was a cold piece of work from what I hear. Did you know he used to beat my momma's ass? That's how they got together. The first time they met, Boss Lady was rocking a black eye. Then the next time he saw her, she bloody, beaten, barefoot, and walking down the street in nothing but a damn nightgown. My father rescued her, and they've been together ever since."

"Uncle Thug a real one for that one. That's similar to my daddy and momma's story. From what I hear, Ace kidnapped my momma and me. If it wasn't for my daddy, ain't no telling where we would be. Grandma Sherita be telling me all about it, and if my momma knew, she would snap. It's like she tries to behave like that shit never happened. What are the odds of Remy Ma's parents both having fucked up biological sperm donors? As pissed off as I am with Dro, I know he won't hurt her. All of this is a move to hurt me for fucking with Yasir.

"Speaking of Yasir, I heard them niggas was humbugging like hell."

"Humbugging ain't the word. Them bitches were fighting like they were both Mayweather. That's how all this shit started. Had I known he would act a fool like this, I never would have gone out that night."

I had to look at her ass like she was crazy.

"Don't do that to yourself, Heaven. It's okay for you to go out and enjoy yourself with your nigga. Dro doesn't get to dictate shit if he over there playing house with someone else. Don't be apologetic for moving on after you waited for that nigga to get his shit together. You deserve happiness, even if it ain't with him. I know how hard it was for you to move on, but that's on him. Don't worry everything is going to be okay."

"I hope so. Yasir is getting tired of the drama, and I can feel it. I've been thinking about calling shit quits just keep confusion down. I'll be single if it means keeping the peace.

"No! Your ass is not calling shit quits! That's what Lil Dro wants, and if you do, you're letting him win. I love Lil Dro, that's my family, and we have all grown up together, but I would rather see you guys co-parent in peace if being in a relationship with him brings you no peace. Yasir has been in love with you since high school. I need for you to let that man love you."

Heaven sat up and looked at me surprisingly.

"What bitch? Why you looking at me like that?"

"Because I can't believe this you talking like this. Where in the hell is my best friend at right now?"

"This is your best friend, but I've lost the love of my life. I didn't appreciate his presence, so now that he's gone I see shit differently. I don't want you missing out on the love of your life behind bullshit. It's not worth it."

"Yasir is a great guy don't get me wrong. Outside of the bullshit with Lil Dro I love how he loves me. It just seems like he is two different people. On one hand he's Yasir I'm trying to build a new life with. On the other hand he's this mysterious nigga that I know nothing about. Do you think I'm overthinking shit?"

"Hell yeah! I've seen how that boy is with you and he loves you. At the same time he's lost his family so he's under pressure. Just embrace it Heaven." She deserved to be happy with Yasir and I was going to do whatever I could to make sure she embraces it.

For the rest of the night, we chilled and ate pizza as we caught up on *Good Girls*. That nigga Rio would have a bitch looking for him with a flashlight. The next morning we woke up to phone calls that Lil Dro had finally come home with the baby, which caused more shit because Remy had beaten his ass. The whole world has seen Lil Dro get his ass beat because Malik taped the shit and uploaded it to Facebook. He so damn messy it don't make any sense, not to mention petty as fuck. This family is dysfunctional as fuck. I'm just happy it's not me in the spotlight this time.

$$\approx$$

Much to my dismay, my family decided to do a gender reveal. These were the most persistent family members in the world, but I loved them for loving me through my pain. I was so ready to go home to my own house. I just didn't know how to tell my daddy. He was adamant about me staying there with them, but all I wanted was my own bed. Plus, Jr. and I needed some peace and quiet. My parents' house was a damn zoo. That added with hearing them fuck all day and all night had me traumatized. I see why Kaia, Kahari, and Kylie basically lived in the game room. It drowns out those weird ass animalistic noises they be making. I'm so tired of my mother walking around naked that I don't know what the hell to do.

I threw up in my mouth a little bit, as I looked at the banana pudding Auntie Sherita had made. I'm almost positive the Nilla Wafers shouldn't have been floating like that. My stomach churned looking at the potato salad that Aunt Gail had made. The potatoes were damn near whole and looked undone. I wished people would stop them from cooking when they're drunk. Thank God, Grandma Peaches stay on point with her food.

For the last hour, I've been fucking up these shrimp bowls she made. Ever since I've been pregnant, all I've craved for is seafood.

"Give me back my damn wig, Malik!" Auntie Barbie yelled as she chased him around the back yard. She was looking like a nigga with French braids to the back.

"Hell nah! I told your ass to stop smacking me upside my head."

Everybody was laughing and having a good time. Sadness came over me as watched my momma and the rest of her girls start chasing Malik. That made my daddy and his crew start chasing them. Just knowing that I'll never grow old with Yahmeen has me on an emotional rollercoaster.

"You good over here, sis?" Kaine asked as he sat next to me.

"I'm trying to be. What about you? Are things good with you and Milania?"

"Shit is good! It's actually the best it has ever been for us."

"Well, I'm glad y'all doing good. Your ass better behave because I know for a fact that girl loves you."

"I used to question her love, but there is no need for me to question her anymore. That's my baby."

Hearing Kaine be so open and free about his love for Milania made me so happy. He is usually the hardcore brother who shows no emotions, so this is a first for me.

"Look at you growing all up on me." I laughed.

"I had to get my shit together before it was too late. The last thing I ever want is to live without Milania and my kids."

I heard Kaine talking, but I had zoned out. Just hearing my brother speak so proudly as a man and a father made me think of Yahmeen. I hated this shit. The simplest of conversations made me think of that man.

"Do you think Yahmeen is dead?" I blurted out the question without even thinking.

"That nigga better be dead because if he ain't, he going to wish the fuck he was! Stop sitting and sulking. Whether that nigga is dead or alive, you and your kids gone forever be straight." He kissed me on the jaw and quickly walked away before I could say anything.

Kaine actually walked away a little too fast for me. Kaine never really showed me that he didn't like Yahmeen, but he also never showed me that he did. I do know that if it's some bullshit behind Yahmeen's disappearance, Kaine is going to kill any and everything moving.

"Come on, Yah-Yah! It's time for you to bust the balloons and see what we're having."

My momma was dancing with excitement. She was so supportive of me having another baby. I laughed because as soon as I pissed her off, she was going to be complaining about me leaving my kids on her.

"Let my daddy pop them."

"Nah! Come on, baby. This is your event and special moment." He came over and grabbed my hand. I was nervous as hell walking over to the huge black balloon my momma was holding.

"I'm going to cry if it's not a girl."

"I don't know what the fuck you crying for. That damn baby should be the one crying. It doesn't have a clue what the hell he's about to be born into."

"Shut up, Malik!" everybody yelled in unison. One would think he would get tired of people telling him to shut up. I honestly think that makes him talk more.

I took a deep breath before popping the balloon. Both blue and pink confetti flew everywhere along with two sonograms.

"Is this a trick balloon or something, ma? It has blue and pink in it."

I kneeled down and picked up the sonogram to look at it. This was my first time actually seeing my sonogram. My momma was so over the top when I went to get the results that she covered my eyes with a blindfold. Now I know why she was so over the top about me having a gender reveal.

"It's twins Yah-Yah!" Ka'Jariea yelled, and the rest of the family joined in.

Every damn body was happy but me. Here I was thinking that I was having one baby and now I'm having two. I just stood in place staring at the sonogram and crying.

"Don't cry, baby! You should be happy," my daddy spoke lovingly as he wrapped his arms around me. Not long after, my mother and my siblings all gathered around and hugged me.

"I'm all by myself. What am I going to do with three kids?"

"Don't worry. Everything is going to be okay." My momma was trying her best to convince me, but I was not convinced.

I was over this whole gender reveal, and I needed to go home. I played it off like everything was cool, and I bounced when everyone wasn't paying attention. I just wanted to be alone with my son and my thoughts in the comfort of my own home. I felt extremely bad about leaving the way I did. I made sure to text my family in the group chat and let them know how sorry and very appreciative I was. Imagine my surprise when they sent me a video of Aunt Sherita and my Auntie Gail doing the Percolator down the Soul Train line. Now, I would have paid to stay and see that.

&

Later that night as I slept soundly cuddled up with my son, I was awakened by being jerked up out of my sleep. Once I was able to focus, I realized there were two people standing over me with all black on. They had on ski masks, so I couldn't see their face. They were both pointing guns at me, and I was scared as fuck.

"Look, there is a safe behind that picture on the wall. It's all yours. Just please don't hurt me or my son. As you can see I'm pregnant."

"Shut the fuck up! Put this shit on her head." It was a female voice, and I couldn't believe some bitches had broken in my house. My son started to cry, and I tried to roll over to grab him, but the other masked intruder grabbed him, not roughly though. I started to cry, and that's when they put the bag over my head.

"Please don't hurt us!" I pleaded.

"Just cooperate, and nothing will happen to either of you. Try some of that tough shit you be on, and it's lights out."

That statement piqued my interest and made me try to think who the fuck these bitches are. It's obvious they know me.

I could feel myself being led out of the house barefoot because I could feel my feet on the concrete. My son was no longer crying, and that helped me to calm down. I was more scared for him than I was for me. A phone started to ring, and one of the women answered and began to speak in Arabic. I immediately started to think about Raja and the fact that I had murked her ass. The shit had really slipped my mind. These had to be her people coming to slaughter my dumb ass. If this was how it ended for me, I was content with that. These bitches have no clue of their fate when my parents get a hold to their ass.

I wanted to badly spazz out and fight their ass, but there was no telling what they would do to us. Feeling myself being placed inside of a car kind of freaked me out, but I remained calm. I was kicking my own ass for being hard headed and leaving my parents' house. For all I know these motherfuckers had been waiting for me to return home.

"Where are you taking us to?"

"Be quiet." The feeling of a gun being pressed to the side of my stomach made me shut the hell up.

We drove for what seemed like hours before we came to a stop. I was happy because I started feeling like I was going to be sick. My baby had fallen asleep. I knew because I could hear him lightly snoring. Moments after the car stopped, I was being pulled out. After a short distance, I could feel myself being led up some stairs. After being led up the stairs, I was roughly pushed down into a seat.

"I'm about to place your son in your arms, and after about ten minutes you can remove the bag from your head. Listen to me and listen to me good. If you try anything, I'll put a bullet in your head and give lil man to a family for adoption. Your best bet is to sit here and be calm until all of this over. "

This bitch was pissing me off so bad at the moment. All I needed was for this hoe to put that gun down, and we could fight head the fuck up. This bitch was doing way too much. I relaxed a little feeling my son being placed into my arms. There were conversations going on in the distance, but I couldn't make out what they were saying.

"We're clear for takeoff!"

I immediately snatched the bag from my head.

"What the fuck is going on? Where are you taking me?"

At this moment, I was panicking like hell. Looking around, I was obviously on a luxury private jet. Looking around, I no longer saw the two people who kidnapped me. Standing to my feet, I quickly rushed to the cockpit, but the door was locked.

"Who the fuck is in here? Do not take off! Let us off of here!"

"Have a seat, Ms. Kenneth. It's not good for you to be up on your feet while the plane is taking off," someone said over the loudspeaker who I presumed to be the pilot.

"I don't care! Let me off this fucking plane! My daddy is going to murder you and your whole family for fucking with me!" I cried, pleaded, and beat on the cockpit door, but the door never opened.

A jerk of the plane caused me to lose my balance and fall with my baby. He had hit his head but not too hard. His cries made me calm down a little. Sitting back in my seat, I cradled my baby and prayed for us to make it out of this shit.

&

"Wake up, Ms. Kenneth. We've landed."

I jumped out of my sleep feeling someone touching my shoulder. I realized it was most likely the pilot. He did have on the uniform, but for all I know, it could just be a trick. After hours of being on a flight to the unknown, I was tired, sleepy, and hungry as fuck, not to mention my baby was wet as hell from not having a change of pamper. I was almost positive that I was going to end up killing this man, especially since the original two bitches who kidnapped me were now nowhere to be seen. Some shit was not right about this whole kidnapping scene.

"Where are we?"

"You're in Maui, Hawaii. It's a beautiful day. Unfortunately, I need to place the bag over your head just until we make it to the final destination."

"I wish you stupid motherfuckers go ahead and kill me. This whole kidnapping scheme y'all got going on is so damn stupid. I swear if I didn't have my baby with me, I would try to kill y'all with my bare hands."

He placed the damn bag over my head while I was still talking. He gently removed my son from my arms.

"Stand up so that we can get off of the plane."

Standing to my feet, a surge of pain shot through my body. It was most likely because I had been sitting down for so long. My legs felt like noodles as I was led off the plane. Once I hit the pavement, my damn feet started to burn from the hot pavement. The smell of fresh air coming through my nostrils relaxed me even if it was momentarily. I wasn't even trying to relish in the fact of being in such a beautiful place like Maui. For all I know, they were leading me to my damn demise.

It wasn't that long of a walk before I was being placed into a car. Exhausted wasn't even a word for the way that I was feeling. The sound of my baby getting fussy angered me. He was hungry and wet as hell. I prayed he was okay because if I was feeling sick, I could only imagine the way he was feeling.

"Please get my baby a bottle and a clean diaper. I don't care what you do to me, just please take care of him.

"No worries, Ms. Kenneth. You and Jr. will be just fine. It won't be long now."

The fact that this man called my son Jr. made my antennas go up instantly. Only family calls my son that name. Something is definitely up with this shit. I didn't want to get ahead of myself, but this shit was not sitting right with me. I wanted to snap on his ass, but I didn't. I decided to play it cooler than I had this entire time.

We drove for what seemed like twenty minutes. Again, I was led out of the car with the bag on my head. As I took slow walks on the hot ass pavement and up about three stairs, I felt myself step into a cooler and more refreshing climate. Beneath my feet, it felt cold, and I knew I was standing inside of a house. I began to shiver. It was just that cold. I felt my baby being removed from my arms and then the bag was removed from my head. My heart sank looking at Yahmeen. My emotions were all over the place looking at him kiss my baby on his forehead.

"I'll take him now, Mr. Yahmeen. Welcome home, Ms. Ka'Jaiyah. We've been waiting on you," a big black woman in a maid's uniform removed my son from his arms and walked away.

I waited until my son was no longer in the room, and I slapped the shit out of him.

"Nigga! You got me so fucked up!"

"Calm down!"

"Bitch, don't tell me to calm down. Take me home right now. I swear to God my daddy and my brothers are going to fuck your lying, deceiving, and conniving ass up. Really nigga? You leave me for dead, and you're out here living a good ass life like shit is sweet. I don't want to hear shit, Yahmeen. I've been struggling without you. In case you give a fuck, I'm pregnant with twins. All I've been doing is crying and trying to cope with not knowing your fate. Obviously, you've been living great while I've suffered. Your best bet is to get me on a plane the fuck out of here!"

"I know that you're mad at a nigga. I'll explain everything when you allow me to. In the meantime, get comfortable we'll be here for a while. Ms. Rosetta will show you to our bedroom."

He tried to walk away, but I quickly grabbed the back of his shirt.

"Where the hell are you going?"

"I have a business meeting to attend. I'll be back later."

"You have me so fucked up, Yahmeen!"

"Calm down and watch your mouth, Yah-Yah! Now, like I said, I'll be back. Please go get cleaned up and get some rest. I'm sorry things have played out this way. I promise I'll tell you everything." Yahmeen rushed out of the door.

I was angry and hurt like hell. The shit had me numb and unable to move. I clenched my fists tight and cried hard as hell. I literally wanted to kill this motherfucker.

"Come on Ms. Yah-Yah. You need to get cleaned up and eat you some dinner."

I stared at this woman and wanted to beat her ass. Before I could even tell her to get the fuck out my face, a wave of sickness rushed over me, and I vomited all over the floor.

"Please give me a phone. I need to call my parents!" I managed to get out in between vomiting. This shit literally had me sick to my stomach.

"I'm sorry, Ms. Yah-Yah, I can't do that. Please come on and let me clean you. It's obvious you're not feeling well. I promise nothing is going to happen to you or Jr. Mr. Yahmeen has been so sad without you and the baby."

I didn't give a fuck about that nigga, but I did need to rest and eat something. All of this shit has drained me, and all I want to do is lie down.

"Where is my son?"

"He's inside the playroom. We can go and check on him before we get you cleaned up. I understand this is hard Ms. Yah-Yah, but Mr. Yahmeen is so nice, and I know he'll make things right."

I wanted to respond to her, but I decided against it. This lady was just doing her job, and I couldn't take my anger out on her even if I wanted to.

I followed her down the long corridor, and she showed me to the playroom. Jr. was having the time of his life playing with the blocks. With him being content, I was okay with leaving him alone to finish playing. Following her down the hall, I became in awe of the beautiful bedroom. It was more like a suite, and it was Chanel themed. Yahmeen knows I'm a Chanel fanatic. This room was bigger than my other rooms back home put together.

"It's beautiful, isn't it? Mr. Yahmeen oversaw the entire project. I'll leave you alone to get cleaned up. You can find everything you need in your closet over there. This is the intercom and security system. You can watch Jr. while you bathe."

She left me alone, and all I could do is look around and wonder why Yahmeen had to leave me alone to do all of this. I feel so betrayed.

Walking inside of the closet it was filled to the brim with nothing but designer shit. This man knows I love wigs by Tae. He even had the nerve to have all styles and colors for my ass. Just looking around it looks like he's definitely trying to make this our home. I instantly got in my feelings because I've never been away from my family. I'm not even thinking about making this place my home because it's not. Yahmeen is going to wish he had gone about this shit better than what he did. My father is going to kill his ass when he finds this shit out.

Getting out of my feelings, I decided just to take a bath and try my best to relax. Being kidnapped and carrying twins was exhausting as fuck. I think I'm really pissed at him about that shit. He could have just brought his ass back to Chicago to get me himself. All of this theatrical shit got me wanting to kill his ass. After running some bath water, I sat inside of the tub, and my body instantly became relaxed. I prayed this helped my aching body because I was in so much pain. I know it comes from all of the events that have transpired. The way I feel scares me because it's too soon to have my babies. They need to stay in the oven and bake a little bit more. For the first time, I embraced being pregnant with twins. Not that I didn't at first, it's just that when I thought I was actually being kidnapped my kids were my only concern. I can't believe my wild ass about to have three kids with this lying ass nigga. Somebody needs to pinch me and wake me up. This shit is definitely a fucking nightmare.

After about thirty minutes of soaking, I finally go out of the tub. As I dried off, I noticed my feet were swollen like pizza puffs. It was imperative that I put my feet up. Climbing into the huge canopy bed, I sank into the down comforter. Moments later the maid came in carrying Jr. He was knocked out.

"Thank you." She handed him to me, and I laid him on my chest.

"He has a nursery that he can sleep in, but I thought you might want him here with you. I made you something to eat. Would you like it now?"

"No thank you. I just really want to sleep. I'm exhausted, and my body hurts. I just need some rest."

"Understandable. I'll let you rest, but when you get up, you have to eat something Ms. Yah-Yah. Mr. Yahmeen just called and asked if you ate anything.

"Fuck Yahmeen! Close the door on your way out." I was just about sick of her Ms. Garrett looking ass talking about Yahmeen.

Lord, I needed to hurry up and get the fuck out of here before I end up killing someone. Granted it wasn't her fault, but she was irritating me. Realizing Jr.'s fat ass was heavy on my chest, I laid him beside me and cuddled under him.

Chapter Sixteen

YAHMEEN

Just seeing Yah-Yah after all of these months had me feeling good as fuck. I didn't even care that she was mad at me. Her presence had a nigga feeling like a motherfucking king. Her being pregnant with my seeds again only made me feel even more powerful than I already am. A nigga had to do what the fuck he had to do. After learning what the fuck my father was up to, I had to become ten steps ahead of him. The nigga was plotting to murder Yah-Yah, and I couldn't let that shit ride. Once I saw Yah-Yah murk Raja, I knew them motherfuckers was going to be coming for my baby.

The only problem was that I never knew he wanted me dead too. The day of the accident, it was my pops who had orchestrated the hit against us. The last thing I remembered was being hit in the back before crashing into the tree. The next thing I know, I'm waking up from a coma a month later out here in Maui. I woke up to no familiar faces. There was nothing but around the clock hospital care until I regained my strength. Imagine my surprise when my brother Yasir showed up. He saved my life, and that was actually surprising to me because I wasn't trusting his ass either. Apparently, he had been following me because he overheard conversations between my father and Raja's father about what to do with me. He wanted me to choose his family, but I chose the family that I was building. In my parents' eyes that was disloyalty, so I had to die.

Learning that my mother agreed with him, it killed the part of me that loved her so much. Yasir did a good job by offing their ass and acting like the mourning son. The best thing that came out of all of this is that I secured my position as head of my father's drug operation prior to Raja being killed. By making him think that I was choosing her, he willingly handed shit over to me. I have everything I want besides Yah-Yah's trust right now, and that's all I need to take this next step with her.

It had been hours since I left her. After my meeting I hauled ass getting back to the crib. I prayed that she likes the room I put together for her. It was pricey getting her all of those wigs her ass loves to rock. Who the fuck knew hair sewed like a damn helmet could be so fucking expensive? Walking into the house, Ms. Rosetta was there to meet me as usual. Hiring had been the best decision I made. The look on her face showed that Yah-Yah had been on a roll.

"That bad, huh?" I tried hiding my laugh, but it was hard to.

"You have some big making up to do. That is no lady back there asleep. She's a Pitbull in a skirt, and you have my prayers. Dinner is on the stove. I'm headed to bed." She shook her as she walked off.

Ms. Rosetta is usually able to handle any task given to her. I knew Yah-Yah was going to be difficult. I was wrong for leaving her in the wrath of storm Yah-Yah, but I had shit to do. Before heading to deal with Yah-Yah, I needed to flame up a blunt and have a shot. A nigga needed calm ass nerves to take on that "Pitbull in a skirt" as Rosetta called her.

"It's good to see you chilling and enjoying life. Did you book my flight back home, Yahmeen?"

Looking up from my shot, Yah-Yah was standing in the dining room with Jr. on her hip. The scowl on her face made her sexy as fuck. She was carrying my son and daughter well. The shit had her looking good as fuck. A nigga couldn't help but lick his lips. Getting up from the bar stool I was sitting on, I walked and took my son from her arms.

"You are home, Ka'Jaiyah."

"It's like you're a glutton for punishment. Do you want me to burn this motherfucker down? Nigga, you know I'm about that life."

"And you know what happens when you try to prove to me that you're about that life. Look, I understand you mad at a nigga, and you should be, but at least let me explain." I tried stroking her face, but she knocked my hand away.

"How could you leave me there alone to die?"

Yah-Yah had tears streaming down her face, and I quickly pulled her into my embrace. It felt so good just to hold her in my arms. A nigga needed a hug more than anything at the moment. In my heart, I know she needed a hug way more than I did. She had no clue that all I had in this world was her and our son outside of Yasir. I no longer had parents, not that I was pressed about it. They made their choice, and I made mine. Ka'Jaiyah Kenneth was my choice.

Grabbing her hand, I led her into the living room so that we could talk. In the end, I hope that she would have a better understanding about things.

"I would never leave you alone like that. A nigga loves your nutty ass more than anything in this world. I woke up a month after the accident at a hospital here in Maui. I had no idea how I got here until a week after I woke up. Yasir showed up and explained everything to me.

"Wait a minute! Yasir knew all along?"

"Yes, but—"

"Now my daddy and brothers are going to beat both of y'all ass! That nigga lied to me about everything."

"Let me stop you right there. Stop saying that disrespectful ass shit. You know ain't no hoe in my blood. Now, do I feel like I owe an explanation to your father? Yes, I do. I want to marry their daughter, so I know I have to have a sit down with that man. However, as far as me getting my ass beat, I don't take that type of shit too light. Now calm your ass down and let me finish what the hell I'm saying.

"You don't have to finish. All I know is it's been seven months, and you woke up after a month. The moment you knew I was left behind, you were supposed to come for me. You knew I was pregnant, not to mention I'm almost sure Yasir told you how sad I've been without you. So yeah! Nigga, you can keep the explanation because that shit is about seven months too late. Please book me a flight home, and that's my last time asking nicely before I start destroying and burning shit." She walked away from me without so much as a blink of an eye.

Yah-Yah had every right to be mad at a nigga, but how could she understand if she doesn't allow me to explain. A part of me wanted just to give her space, but we had been a part long enough. She could be stubborn all she wanted to, but I was going to make shit right no matter what.

"Da Da!" To hear my son call me that was like music to my ears. I hadn't heard his voice in so long. Kissing him on the forehead, I headed to the bedroom to try and talk to Yah-Yah again. I couldn't sleep another night without her.

My intentions were to burst inside the room and start demanding that she listen, but hearing her loudly crying made me stop in my tracks. Yah-Yah was not the typical woman who cried just so she would get her way. She was more so a person who got mad and did petty shit in order to get her way. The way she was crying, you would think someone had died. My baby was hurt, and I had hurt her. A nigga needed to fix this immediately because I didn't go through everything I did just to end up losing her. It was a good thing I had a Plan B because Yah-Yah wasn't going to make this shit easy on a nigga. This needed to be rectified fast because all of this crying and these emotions couldn't be healthy on her or the babies. I would never forgive myself if the stress I've put on her were the cause of something happening to her or our kids.

It wasn't easy getting on the phone and hitting up Thug, but he was my last hope in regards to making shit straight all the way around. The moment I called him, he hopped on a flight out to Maui but made me promise not to say anything to Yah-Yah. He didn't have to worry about that because she locked herself in the bedroom and said she wasn't coming out until I booked her flight. I don't understand why she doesn't get that I'm not getting her no fucking flight home. Sitting across from my brother, I could tell he was feeling some type away about me reaching out to Thug. He wasn't speaking on it, but I could feel his energy.

"What's good, bro? You've been quiet since you sat down."

I flamed up a fat ass blunt and passed it to him. The look on his face was some shit I really didn't care for. Clearly he had an issue, and he needed to address that shit because this was going to be my last time asking what the fuck was up with him.

"Do you really think it was necessary to call Thug out here?"

"Hell yeah! He's the only one who can talk some sense into Ka'Jaiyah. That added with the fact that I need to talk to that man anyway. In case you forgot our family drama has affected the fuck out of Yah-Yah. My absence had her people doing what the fuck I was supposed to be doing for her."

This nigga had me looking at him like he was crazy as hell. I couldn't believe he thought it wasn't a good idea for me not to all Thug.

"I understand all of that. I just feel like some shit needs to be handled accordingly. We got our own money, and we don't need to answer to any motherfucking body."

"Bro, this doesn't have shit to do with that man's money. This is about the respect I have to give that man because I want to marry his daughter, not to mention I hurt Yah-Yah. It might not have been intentional, but I hurt her. In case you forgot, I had her and my son kidnapped. I have to holla at that man behind that shit. You think we can just keep moving weight without beef if I don't talk to him. Thug and his crew aren't no regular ass niggas."

"You sound like them niggas God or some shit! I honestly don't see why you want to marry her ass anyway. Every time she doesn't get her way she's going to throw a tantrum and fuck up your life. Keep bowing down to her, and your ass gone be wearing the panties, and she's going to be slinging the dick."

"You're my brother, and I love you, but make that your last mother-fucking time disrespecting me and who the fuck I am. Don't think because you helped me get my health back and the ball running with the family business that I'm taking any shit from you. Don't ever disrespect Ka'Jaiyah like that. How I handle her is not your concern, lil nigga. Focus on being Heaven's second choice."

I stood the fuck up and walked out on his ass. That venom he had just spit had me seeing red. Yasir was all the fuck I had, and I needed the support of my family. For him to be sitting up with that type of shit got my ass thinking hard about Yah-Yah being left behind that day. I needed to have this meeting with Thug, and I would deal with his ass later. The shit he's on got me rethinking a lot of the moves we made. People don't talk like that out of the blue. That nigga has been had that shit on his heart.

❧

It wasn't a surprise seeing both Thug and Ms. Tahari. I should have known she was going to be right with him. I think she did pump a little fear in a nigga. I've seen her in action, and she is nothing to fuck around with, especially when it comes down to her kids. I had them meet me at the Palm Beach Grill, which happens to be one of the best restaurants in Maui. They were both knocking back shots, and I'm glad that I had some shots before arriving. Hopefully, the situation would be calmer.

"Thanks for coming on such short notice."

"Cut the bullshit! Where the fuck is my daughter and grandson?" Ms. Tahari wasted no time going in on my ass. Thug, on the other hand, just sat staring with a scowl on his face. I'm positive his ass had a gun on his lap.

"This is not a social call. What the fuck is good?"

"I'm going to get right to it. All of this shit got out of control from the moment my father put a hit out on Yah-Yah. At first, I never knew he didn't care for her. It wasn't until after the birth of Jr. that he started shifting. All of a sudden, I was no longer allowed to marry Yah-Yah, and I had to marry Raja. From that moment on, I knew I was done with my parents. I just never knew it was so serious that they would try to kill her.

With Yah-Yah and I being on the outs I decided to seize the opportunity to become head of my father's organization. In order for me to do that, I had to agree to marry Raja. He was more than willing to hand it over. I just needed him to trust me. With that part squared away, I thought shit was cool. It all went left when he decided to pay Yah-Yah to stay away from me and hand over custody of Jr. That sent her off, and she murked Raja, which made both she and I wanted by Raja's people. Once I found out what happened, I immediately rushed to the crib and came clean to her about everything. Once we made shit right we were headed to y'all crib. I wanted to let you all know everything, but in route, the car was shot up. The next thing I know I woke up here in Maui in a hospital recovering. Finally, my brother Yasir showed up and told me about the death of my parents and how I ended up here.

Instead of me rushing to come back to the Chi, I stayed here and got some business affairs in order. With my father being dead, I am now head of the family business. I'm sorry that I placed Yah-Yah in such a bad spot, but I love her more than anything in this world. That's why I had to stage a kidnapping to get her and my son here with me. She wouldn't have been able to understand had I just shown up and tried to get her to come with me."

"Either you love my daughter, or you don't like your life!" Thug spoke as he knocked back the drink he had.

"I love my life and your daughter. That's why I'm sitting here now. Yah-Yah is back at the estate, and she's not trying to hear anything I have to say. I called you because I'm ready to marry her. All I have is her and my kids. She might not believe me, but a lot of decisions I've made was for us. I feel like if she sees y'all she'll calm down. All she keeps doing is cursing me out and threatening to burn the house down if I don't put her on a flight back to Chicago. I lost her once, and I can't do that again."

A nigga had to put it all out there in the name of love. Some may call the shit soft but fuck that. Gangsters need love too, and this gangsta needs Yah-Yah. My baby momma is definitely harder than a lot of these niggas, and I need her riding shotgun with me for the rest of my life.

"The only reason I haven't killed you is because I truly believe you love my daughter. The last nigga I murked behind fucking with my daughter is on a missing person's poster, so no one is exempt when it comes to my seeds. I'm a good judge of character, and I know you love my daughter. That and the fact that anyone who goes so hard for Ka'Jaiyah Kenneth has got to be in love with her. I'm her father, and the shit is not easy."

"I love how you love my daughter. I'll support trying to get her to come around, but on only one condition."

"You name it Ms. Tahari."

"If she wants to come back to the Chi and live then you have to allow that to happen. I'm never going to force her to be in a place that she's unfamiliar with. All she knows is Chicago. This scene may be paradise, but it will be a prison to her if she's unhappy. Trust me. Both my husband and I know firsthand about what you're dealing with in regards to family and doing shit to stay ahead for the sake of love. For some reason, you and my daughter reminded me of us."

"If going back to Chicago will make her happy, then that's where we would be. Whatever Yah-Yah wants she gets, anything to keep her from burning another house down."

"Take me to the estate. I need to see her and my grandson. "

Ms. Tahari stood to her feet, and I observed her placing her gun in her Birkin bag.

"Don't look shocked. I told you I keep it on me. Let's go." I looked at Thug and shook my head.

"Don't shake your head at me. Get prepared for your future with my daughter. Yah-Yah is from my loins, but Boss Lady birthed her." We laughed, and all headed towards the house.

I just prayed Yah-Yah wanted to stay here in Maui. I busted my ass trying to get that house just right for her. At the same time, I have enough money to do the same thing back home. I'm a rich ass nigga these days, so money is not an issue.

Chapter Seventeen

YAH-YAH

I was so happy Ms. Rosetta and Yahmeen had left the house finally. They were both irritating me like hell trying to talk to me. That nigga had me fucked up if he thought I was giving in just because he was saying sorry. I'm making his ass sweat just like he did me. I know motherfucking well he didn't think I was going to let teaching me a lesson slide. I'm keeping that same fucking energy with him that he had with me. Keeping up this damn game is hard as fuck though. That nigga look so fucking good to me that it don't make any sense.

The last time we made love, it was everything. The shit was so good that he got my ass pregnant with twins. To make matters worse, he be walking around smelling good as fuck with that Versace cologne on. These babies have my hormones through the roof. One minute I want to take the dick, and the next I want to murder his ass. I've basically locked myself in the bedroom and only coming out when I know no one is in the house. At first, I was starving myself, but my babies wasn't having that shit. No matter how mad I am with Yahmeen, I'm so happy he's not dead.

My son deserves his daddy. No, let me rephrase, that my kids deserve their father. I'm literally starting to see that he be trying to move mountains for my petty stubborn ass. It's his fault this time around though. He should have come for me sooner and not kidnapping me. That shit had me scared and helpless as fuck. I'm mad because I suffered and it seems like he was living. I do take it into consideration that he put things in place for us to live a better life. At the same time, I'm so angry that he allowed me to think the worse.

As I stood in the kitchen, I could hear Yahmeen pull into the driveway. My baby was already sleep so I rushed to the bedroom and got in bed next to him. I closed my eyes and played sleep in the hopes that Yahmeen wouldn't try talking to me. Hearing the door open, I clenched my eyes tight.

"Wake up, Yah-Yah! Your ass is not sleep." The sound of my mother voice made me quickly sit up.

"Ma! I'm so happy to see you. Where is daddy? How did you know that I was here?" I swear I was trying my best not to cry, but I it was hard. She hugged me tight and then placed a kiss on my son cheek.

"He went to handle some business with Yahmeen."

"What type of business?" My mind started racing hearing her say that.

"Don't worry he's fine. Sit down so we can talk."

Hesitantly, I sat back down on the bed so that we can talk. I could only imagine what she was about to say to me. Thinking of my father being out with Yahmeen had me scared as fuck. Knowing my daddy, he probably really was kicking his ass for kidnapping me and shit.

"Your father and I are here because Yahmeen called us. He explained everything to us Yah-Yah. You need to hear him completely out without acting like a brat. That man went against his blood for you. The least you can do is give him that."

"So, you agree with what he did to me?"

"Don't put words in my mouth. I don't agree with you being left behind to die. That wasn't on that man. At the same time, when he came to, he was supposed to reach out for you. Trust me. I understand your hurt and frustration. In case you have forgotten, your father had a whole funeral and was gone from me a whole year. I was pregnant, and that was the worse time of my life. When I finally saw your father, I was so pissed that it made no sense. After all that I had been through, how could he just be living life while I was suffering. During that time,

I wasn't Boss Lady. I was simply his Ta-Baby. Your dad took me through it, but I always knew I wanted to be with him. Thug could go out and get any woman he wants but chooses me. I look at Yahmeen, and the boy chooses you. He lost his family because he chose you.

Now I won't tell you to stay somewhere you don't want to, but I will say give this Maui thing a try, not to mention this relationship. A man like Yahmeen comes a dime a dozen. Don't let your pride have him choosing someone else."

"I would kill him and that bitch! Excuse my language, but I'm not even having it, ma."

"Well keep sitting up in this room avoiding him, and that's exactly what's going to happen. Get dressed and let's go shopping or something. This place is beautiful and you're sitting here in this room in the dark. It would do you some good to get some damn sun. You look pale to me. Are you eating like you're supposed to? I understand that you've been all depressed and shit, but you need to make sure you eat properly. Carrying twins will drain you, so you absolutely have to eat. Stop all this stressing and try to get those babies as close to term as possible. You've passed the six month mark so that's really good."

I watched as she opened the curtains and let some sun inside. The palms trees in the backyard swayed as the wind blew lightly. I had to admit to myself that Yahmeen had definitely outdone himself with this house. It was absolutely perfect. Our homes back home were nothing compared to this place.

"I'm getting my tubes tied after this. These babies are taking me through it. I wasn't prepared to be a mother of three so early in life. I love being a mom, but Yahmeen is not about to have my pretty ass walking around like a little old lady in a shoe."

"I said the same thing, and every time your daddy looked at me I was pregnant." We both laughed.

"Well, I'm going to blind Yahmeen's ass because I can't do it."

We both laughed, and the sound of the garage opening made both of us head down the stairs. As soon as I made it to the bottom step, I saw my daddy. My ass almost fell trying to get to him.

"Daddyyyy! I'm so happy to see you."

"Calm down. You okay?"

It felt so good being in my father's arms. Just seeing him made me feel so much better. Looking over his shoulder, I locked eyes with Yahmeen. He looked at me but quickly walked away. He had called my parents because I missed them and wanted to go home.

"Yeah, I am. I just miss y'all, that's all."

"Well, you're in good hands, Ka'Jaiyah. From the looks of this house, life is great, and from what Yahmeen has told me, it will be better. You need to go and talk with Yahmeen. Let me spend some time with my grandson before your mother and I hop back on this flight home. We have some business we need to handle that can't be put off. Right now is when you decide if you're going to leave with us or stay here with the father of your children. I support whatever you want to do."

"Really daddy? Y'all just got here and leaving already. Momma and me were about to go shopping."

"The last thing either of you need is to go shopping. We have an important business meeting that we can't miss." He kissed me on the forehead and went over to where my mom was at holding Jr.

I was apprehensive about approaching Yahmeen. I had been so mean and hard on his ass that I didn't know if he would even want to talk to me. It was now or never for our relationship. He went out of his way to get my parents here. The best thing I could do is give him the chance to explain. Actually, I no longer want an explanation. He has apologized in more ways than one. Walking inside his man cave, I observed him sitting in his chair. His head was leaned back, and he was staring at the ceiling in deep thought.

"I just wanted to let you know that I'm going to stay here with you."

"Are you sure that's what you want to do? The last thing I need is for you to feel like I'm pressuring you to be here. If you want to go back home with your parents, I understand. Just please understand that we share children. No matter how you feel about me, I have a say so when it comes down to my kids."

"You're right. That's why I'm staying. Being pregnant and alone has taken a toll on me, not to mention Jr. missed you so much. I wouldn't dream of walking away now that I know you're alive and well. I've just been so pissed off at you that I couldn't really embrace how grateful I am that you're okay. Forgive me for being emotionally unavailable in a moment where we needed each other."

He stood and walked over to me. Without hesitation, I wrapped my arms around his neck and we engaged in a passionate kiss. My body melted into him. This was literally the first time in months I felt him.

"I love you, Yah-Yah."

"I love you too, Yahmeen." My babies started moving around like crazy.

"I guess they're happy we made up too."

"Let me go out here and let my parents know my decision. They have to get back to Chicago," I spoke somberly.

"Don't be sad. I promise in a couple of weeks we can catch a flight out. We can stay out there until after you give birth. Let me handle some business I have here, and then we're good. We can stay out there as long as you like." He kissed my forehead and answered a phone call that was coming through his line.

My parents were sitting on the sofa playing with Jr. Staring at them for a minute, I could only hope to look that damn good when I get their age. Despite everything that they've been through, they both have aged gracefully.

"Thank you guys so much for coming to check on me. I decided I'm staying here with Yahmeen. In a couple of weeks, we will flight out to stay until after I give birth to the babies."

"I'm glad you guys were able to come to a decision that makes both of you happy," my father spoke proudly as he came over and hugged me.

"Yes, I agree and we're proud of you. We love you and we can't wait for you guys to come home. While you're out here in paradise, make sure to make up for all of the lost time." Momma winked her eye, and my daddy shook his head at her. Here I was pregnant again, and he still wasn't feeling me and the whole sex thing.

For the next hour or so, we talked before their flight left. Their presence made me feel so much better. I'm so glad my mother and I have built a better bond over the last couple of months. I honestly had missed her as much as I missed my father. With them being gone, it was time for me to step up and be the woman Yahmeen wants me to be.

I think I've given him hell long enough.

&.

Later that night, we laid in bed intertwined in each other's arms. The sound of his phone going off piqued my interest. I watched as he purposely ignored. In a minute I was going to grab it just to see if it was a bitch. We were going to break up just as fast as we made up because I had every intention of tap dancing on his motherfucking head.

"Why you not answering the phone?"

"I'm spending time with my family, and I don't want any interruptions."

"It's okay. It might be important." It was odd for him not to answer calls. I wasn't going anywhere, so it was perfectly okay for him to answer.

"It's Yasir, and he don't want shit."

I wanted to ask were they cool but I decided to mind my business. Something was definitely wrong between them. Yahmeen and Yasir have been joined at the hip from the moment I met them. This is the first time I've ever seen Yahmeen ignore Yasir calls.

"I'm sorry if I ruined your family." Although I know that I hadn't done anything to them, I felt like he lost them because they didn't care for me. Before I came into the picture, they were extremely close. I realized later that they were snakes. The story Yasir told me when I arrived at his parent's house was totally different from the story he told Yahmeen. Something was off. At the same time, my family is everything to me and can never imagine living without them. So, no matter what has happened I know he's fucked up behind it.

"You didn't do shit to them. We had our issues and that was our business. My father had no right to come at you like that, and my mother was wrong for being on bullshit with them. I'm hurt behind all of this but there is nothing I can do about it at this point. They made their choice, and I made mine. You don't have to apologize for their behavior. The best apology that I can receive from you is changed behavior and becoming the woman I need you to be."

"You're right, and I attend on working on my anger and the way I go about handling things. Yahmeen, you don't have to put on a brave face for me. I know that you're hurt behind all of this. I just want you to know that I'm here if you need me." I kissed his lips, and he laid his head in my lap.

"I'm fine, Yah-Yah. I just want you to kick back relax and get ready for my seeds to be born."

"Lord knows I'm so ready to get these babies out of me so that I can get my tubes tied."

I threw that last part in there to see his reaction but he kept his game face on and didn't feed into my bullshit. I'm almost positive as soon as I give birth and request to get my shit tied he's going to go ballistic. Looking down at Yahmeen, he was dozing off. He looked exhausted. His phone started going off again, and I prayed nothing was wrong. At the same time, I didn't want him to wake up. He looked so peaceful. Reaching over on the nightstand, I cut the phone completely off so he could get some much needed rest.

The next morning I woke up and tried to cook breakfast but of course, Ms. Rosetta already had the food done. She had Jr. dressed and in a high hair feeding him oatmeal. He would usually cry when I walk into a room, but when Ms. Rosetta around, he don't pay me a lick of attention.

"I wanted to cook Yahmeen breakfast this morning."

"Girl please, you don't look like you do nothing but look pretty and cause chaos. Now sit on down over there so that I can fatten you up."

"Well, at least let me go and wake him up so that we can eat together."

"Mr. Yahmeen doesn't wake up until about ten. He likes his food piping hot, so I usually make his when I know he's showering."

I felt kind of bad because these are things that I should know about him already. Staring at Ms. Rosetta, she reminded me so much of Marta. That lady knows my father better than his own mother.

"I'm glad I know that now. Thanks for telling me." She placed some grits, egg whites, and sausage in front of me.

"You should always know what your man likes and don't like. That's how you keep him happy and satisfied. Even though I get paid to make sure this household is in order, as a future wife, you have to have your shit together. Don't get caught slipping. That's the best way to end up beating Shirley's ass for cooking in your kitchen."

"Who is Shirley?"

"Keep walking around here playing crazy like Barbara and you'll find out."

I was lost as to what she was saying, so I started eating. I didn't have time for Rosetta and her madness this morning. The sound of the doorbell ringing interrupted me from eating.

"Who the hell is that at this door?"

"Sit down and finish eating. I'll get it."

As she was rushing towards the door whoever it was started banging on the door. That made me follow her to see who the hell it was.

"Where the fuck is my brother at?" Yasir almost knocked Ms. Rosetta down trying to get inside of the house.

"Hello to you too, Yasir. He's asleep."

"I'm woke, babe. Take Jr. upstairs while we talk. Ms. Rosetta, you can take the rest of the morning off. I'll call you if I need you. "

Yasir's rude ass had basically woke him up. The scowl on his face was something I had never seen on him before. I guess he was mad that Yahmeen hadn't answered the phone for him. Last night I had a bad feeling that he would be pissed. Looking at Yahmeen, he had a nonchalant look on his face like he was aggravated. This whole scene made me want to call Heaven to see what was good with this nigga. In that moment I realized that I was so caught up in my own madness we hadn't spoken.

Heading up the stairs, I heard them began to argue. Of course, my nosey ass sat at the top of the stairs to hear their conversation. Something was wrong, and I could feel it.

"What's good, bro? I've been calling you all night. Why the fuck you haven't answered for me?"

"Stop yelling, bro. I was exhausted last night. Plus, I just wanted to chill with my family. What was so important that you had to tear my line down like that? I thought you were headed back to the Chi yesterday?"

"I was but some shit came up that I needed to handle. You should have answered the phone, and you would have known that I secured that deal with Otto's fat ass. His team now works for us out here."

"Otto and I already discussed that deal and we came up with a mutual agreement, Yasir! We need that Maui connection for the fucking Meth labs. Why would you go behind me and do some shit like that?"

"Cause that deal was bullshit! I needed him to know he don't run shit out here. Pops allowed him to run it. He's reign is over and a new reign just started!"

"This they shit out here! It doesn't matter if pops gave it to him or not. With us being over shit now, we still need to keep all connections with other territories to keep the money flow going. I gained that nigga's trust and you went behind me and fucked it up! You can't be going behind my back and doing shit like that, bro!"

"Had you not been up laid up under ya bitch you would have known what the fuck I was on! Ever since you brought her out here, you've been on this soft ass shit!"

"Call her another bitch! Watch I shoot you, bro!"

"Really? You gone kill me for her!"

"What the fuck are you talking about? I'm not choosing anybody over you! At the same time, you in my crib disrespecting the mother of my children like I'm some fuck nigga. This shit has nothing to do with her. This shit is about you doing shit without me. If I didn't answer my phone, you should have waited. Your ass is reckless, and the next time you do some shit like that, you're on your own!"

"Get that gun out of my face! Remember, the status you got, I helped you with it! It's because of me you're alive! Don't try to son me! The next time you pull a gun on me, you better use it. Pops was right about you, nigga! You would go against the grain for her. I won't be surprised if you end up being a part of her people organization."

The sound of the door slamming made me rush up the stairs to the room. I didn't want Yahmeen to catch me listening. The sound of glass breaking made me put Jr. in his playroom and rush down stairs. Yahmeen had picked up a barstool and thrown it through the patio door. It broke my heart to see him sitting on the couch rocking back and forth. The fact that he was tapping the gun against his head scared me. During the course of our relationship, I've never seen him in such a stage.

Rushing over to him, I dropped down to my knees in front of him. Out of fear that the gun might accidentally go off, I pried it out of his hands and slid it across the floor. I held him tight as I could. This shit had me heated because his family was hurting him for loving me, and this shit is not fair. I never saw this type of shit from Yasir though. That nigga always came off like he really fucked with me. That venom he spit today made me want to cut his fucking tongue out.

"What the fuck they want from me?" Hearing my nigga voice crack had me seeing red. I don't give a fuck what I do to him, can't nobody else do a motherfucking thing to him.

"Fuck what they want! Don't you dare let a motherfucker make you feel bad about building your life and being here for your family. All of them are wrong as fuck for the way they've came at you for simply loving me. Yeah, I'm a handful, and I understand them not caring for me. However, they all should respect what you want! Look at me, Yahmeen! Don't let that shit take you out of your element! Fuck what he said about me. I'm surprised he feels that way, but at the same time, he don't have to like me. What the fuck he won't do is dismantle your family business that you rightfully inherited. While you're sitting here thinking about this bullshit, you need to be meeting with that nigga to fix what your brother possibly fucked up. You want me to go with you? Pregnant and all I'll ride for you, die for you, right hand in the sky for you, if it came down to it. I don't give a fuck about nothing but being here for you. You're a gangsta, and I'm not accepting anything less from you. I promise I got you forever, baby!"

I leaned my forehead against his and we literally just stared in each other's eyes. No words needed to be spoken. He knew what the fuck he had to do.

"I love you Ka'Jaiyah, and one day I promise to make up for everything."

"You don't have shit to make up for. Yahmeen, you've been more than everything I need in a man. Right now, I need you to go out there and solidify yourself as that new nigga in the streets. Whether we're here or in the Chi, you need to apply pressure. Not just with niggas in the streets, but with Yasir as well. No matter how he feels about me, he needs to understand your name holds weight. I don't give a fuck if he is your brother because he gives me vibes like your father. Watch him."

"I'm already knowing. Come here. Let me show you something." He helped me up from the floor and took me to a panel. He keyed in a code, and a door opened.

"What is this?"

"The gun room. That side is mine. This side is yours. Pick two so I can lock this bitch back up."

My pussy got wet looking at all the pink, purple, and iced out guns. This nigga knew the way to my heart. If I didn't know anything in this world, I knew about this shit. My daddy never allowed his girls to just jump rope and shit like that. He had us in the basement doing target practice. I grabbed the iced out Glock 36 and the hot pink Sig Sauer P226.

"I love these, Yahmeen." He quickly put the code in and locked it up. Examining the guns, they were already locked, loaded, and ready to go.

"Pay attention to what I'm about to say. I wanted you to get those guns in the event you need to protect yourself. Don't ask any questions you shoot to kill if anybody comes through that door or if you're out in the streets without me. I know you know how to hold your own, but I still have to protect you. The code is the day we met. Put them guns in a place that's reachable. I'm about to go and get up with this nigga to have a sit down. I pray Yasir haven't fucked shit up. This meth out here is the real thing. The shit is lucrative as fuck. We can't afford to lose this nigga Otto."

"I'm good, Yahmeen. Go ahead and do what you have to do. We'll be okay. Be careful, and I'll be here when you get back." I stroked his face and kissed him passionately. He rushed away from me and up the stairs.

Sitting down on the couch I kept looking at the guns in my hands and my trigger finger was itching. I was pissed because Yasir had come and really fucked up the energy in our house. Pissed wasn't a word for the way this nigga had me feeling behind fucking with Yahmeen. If I didn't know anything, I know he loved his parents and his brother. For all of them to treat him this way has me livid as fuck! His parents lucky they're already dead, but this nigga Yasir got me seeing red.

About twenty minutes later Yahmeen came down the stairs dressed in all black looking good as fuck.

"I'm about to head out and I might not be back until late. Put the alarm on and keep the security system on in the bedroom so that you can see the perimeter. No one is coming here, I just want you to be on point. I'll send Ms. Rosetta to stay in here with you instead of the guesthouse while I'm gone. Keep your phone by you at all times. Okay, Ka'Jaiyah?"

"Yes, Yahmeen! I hear you. Be careful. I love you."

"I love you too." We passionately kissed and he rushed out the door.

My heart was racing, and I didn't like the shit one bit. I hated being out here in Maui and not knowing anything or anyone. I felt like a sitting duck. Sitting back down on the couch, I jumped hearing the door opened. I settled down seeing that it was Ms. Rosetta.

"Are you okay?"

"Yeah, I'm fine. I'm just worried about Yahmeen. His brother really came over here and upset him. "

"He rubs me the wrong way. I went over to his house to clean for him and the whole time he talked to himself. He kept arguing with some chick named Heaven over the phone. The poor thing needs to leave him alone. With the trash that he had laying up with him, I would be afraid to sleep with him after her. I'm telling you he is off. He behaves one way in front of Mr. Yahmeen and completely different when he's not around him. I'll never go back and clean for him again."

Hearing Ms. Rosetta speak so clearly, I decided I needed more.

"Yasir has a house out here?"

"Oh yes! They have a lot of property out here. Their father left them so many properties all over the place. The house that Yasir stays in was supposed to be their retirement home. The address is over their on the fridge. I never removed it when I wrote it down."

The wheels in my head started to turn, but I couldn't let it be obvious. Ms. Rosetta didn't miss a beat, so I knew she would catch on. I had a plan, but I needed to move with caution. That nigga Yasir was gone have to see me. I needed to address his ass because he had me fucked up, not to mention my family and my friend Heaven. He was playing with my bitch's heart, and she didn't deserve that.

As I sat and thought about it more, I wanted to call Heaven and ask her some questions. Then again, I couldn't do that because she might try to talk me out of it. Yahmeen was going to be mad, but I had to do this. The feeling of my babies moving around reminded me that my ass was pregnant and needed to sit the fuck down. Going to see Yasir would possibly mean putting their lives in danger. I would never forgive myself if something bad happened. For the first time, I'm going to listen to Yahmeen and wait for him to come back home. As bad as I wanted to go and fight that nigga Yasir, I knew that I couldn't. That added with the fact that I didn't even know the ins and outs of Maui. Going to fuck up Yasir would be like a suicide mission, and my crazy ass was not ready to go out like that.

It was still early in the day I so I decided just to chill and wait for Yahmeen to come back home. I tried reaching out to Heaven just to check on her, but her phone was going to voicemail. My ass needed to hurry up and get back to the Chi. My girl needed me. I can just feel it. Between Lil Dro and Yasir, with the bullshit, they're going to have my girl in the nut house. Another reason I want to get back to Chicago is to have my people on deck. That bullshit Yasir was speaking makes me uncomfortable as fuck being out here while he's here. I needed to get that nigga back on my turf and make his ass eat every word. I was trying my best not to worry about Yahmeen, but the shit was so hard. I knew my nigga was good though. There is no way he's not coming home to his Yah-Yah.

"Ms. Rosetta, I'm going to take a nap can you keep an eye on Jr. for me?"

"Absolutely. Get you some rest. I'm going to take him to the park for a little while and keep him at the guesthouse with me. Call when you wake up and I'll bring him right over."

"Thank you. I really appreciate how helpful you've been since we've arrived. I apologize for the way I behaved with you." She still helped me no matter how mean or smart-mouthed I became with her.

"No problem. I would be mad as hell. I'm just glad your mean ass made up with Mr. Yahmeen. Your ass was running my blood pressure up. Get you some rest. We'll be just fine."

As I headed upstairs and walked past the floor length mirror, I caught a glimpse of my full body. I was fat as fuck. My legs and feet were huge. I don't know where the fuck I thought I was going trying to confront Yasir, my big ass would have fucked around and gone in labor. Just looking at how huge I am, it's looking like I won't be able to make it to nine months. If I do, it would be a miracle. Climbing up in the bed, I made sure to send a quick text to Yahmeen telling him that I love him and to be careful. When he responded immediately, I breathed a sigh of relief. That alone helped me to fall asleep better. He needed to hurry up and come back home. At first, I was all for us staying here in Maui for a couple of weeks, but I'm ready to go now. I don't trust being out here any longer.

The smell of Yahmeen's Versace cologne invaded my nostrils as I slept peacefully. It instantly made me sit up and look around for him. It was pitch black in the room. That means my ass had literally slept the day away. I started feeling around for my phone and couldn't find it. The light came on, and that's when I observed Yasir waving my phone around.

"Looking for something?"

"What the fuck are you doing here? Yahmeen!" I yelled and tried to get out of bed, but Yasir pulled a gun on me.

"Sit your ass down. There ain't no need to be calling my brother because he's not here, remember! You told him to go out and be a gangsta." He started laughing wildly, and it was clear this nigga was crazy. He must have had cameras or a recorder in the house to know I told him that.

I decided to try and play it cool without letting this motherfucker know that he was scaring me Quiet as it's kept I was scared as hell. At the same time, I needed to know what the fuck was good with him.

"What the fuck is your issue? Why are you around here doing all of this snake shit? I thought we were cool. Now you're walking around like I did something to you. Just months ago I was your sis, and now you're mad at Yahmeen for choosing me."

"You ruined our family! Before he got involved with your ass, we were good. That nigga said fuck our family for the sake of your ass!"

"I didn't ruin anything. If you want to be technical about it, your father ruined your family when he tried to make him marry that bitch, not to mention pay me to never speak with Yahmeen again!"

"My brother was my best friend before you came into the picture! Now, all of a sudden your people want him to join their team and shit. I hear you telling him how the fuck to move in regards to our business. You came in and fucked up everything! Why the fuck couldn't you just go away?"

He aimed the gun at me, and I put my hands up in defense. I was regretting placing the guns Yahmeen gave me behind the pillows on the sofa so that Ms. Rosetta couldn't see them. Thinking of Ms. Rosetta I was happy she had took my baby home with her.

"Put the gun down, Yasir! What about Heaven and Yahmeen?"

"I love Heaven honestly, but unlike my brother, I choose my blood over bitches. To keep it real we never would have worked anyway. I got her on tape fucking her baby daddy in our crib so, yeah it's a wrap!" Before I could respond, Yahmeen walked inside the room with his gun aimed at Yasir.

"Bro, don't make me do it! You mad at me, not her." Yasir started going off and waving the gun around like he was crazy.

"I killed our parents for you nigga and you don't give a fuck! I 'm the reason why you're here now. I left this bitch in the car for a reason. Don't you get it, nigga! She could never be a part of the family business we have, but you bring her out here, and you're right back to choosing this bitch! "

"Bro, I don't want to kill you! Put that gun down, my nigga!" Yahmeen spoke as tears streamed down his face and that made me cry too. It shouldn't be this way.

"Both of y'all stop this shit. Put the guns down. I'll walk away Yasir, but you don't want to do this!"

I was pleading and trying to get him to calm down, but the moment the words left my mouth, his eyes turned black. That's when I saw the flash of the gun followed by more gunshots. When the smoke cleared, I was in such shock that I didn't realize that I had been hit in the shoulder, and Yasir was slumped over the bed dead. Yahmeen stood holding the gun in shock. Despite the pain in my shoulder, I had to make him snap out of his trance. I slowly walked over to Yahmeen, and with each step, I felt like I was pissing on myself. My water had broken, and I was starting to bleed profusely from the wound in my shoulder.

"Baby, I'm hit. You have to get me to the hospital. We have to gooooo!"

"I fucked up!"

"Noooo! You did what you had to do. Look at me! We have to go nowwwww! The babies are coming!" The last thing I remember was falling into his arms and him carrying me bridal style out of the house.

EPILOGUE

Yahmeen

That saying is true when they say that life can change within the blink of an eye. Life as I knew it changed without warning and out of the blue. One minute I had a mother, father, and a brother, and the next they were all gone, and it seems as though they never existed. It feels pretty fucked up that the life I grew to know is gone because I chose to build a family of my own. Never in a million years did I ever think I would have to murk my brother. He was absolutely in the wrong, but my heartaches behind pulling that trigger.

I'm still so lost as to where it all went wrong. One minute we were the best of friends and the next enemies. My love for Ka'Jaiyah Kenneth had them so threatened. I realize it had nothing to do with her. It was more so about where she came from. Yah-Yah wasn't a threat. It was her family that they were threatened by. Her people had no interests in what my family had going on. We both respected each other's blocks and territories. Looking back, I now realize Yasir was the one who had put shit in my father's head. He planted the seed and orchestrated the hit. It's like everything has been coming back to me. He changed the moment I spoke on us leveling up. It wasn't that he didn't want to. He just wanted to be the one in charge. I felt that shit, but I looked over it because I never thought in a million years that shit would have played out the way that it did.

The only thing I regret behind this shit is not being on point and seeing that he was indeed an enemy. If a motherfucker ever thought I was choosing them over Yah-Yah, then I'm glad shit played out the way it did. They're all dead, and she's still here. Don't get me wrong. I'll always remember the good times that I had with my family. However, the fuck shit that they pulled made me put their ass in the back of my mind. I couldn't dwell on it if I wanted to anyway. I have a wife and kids to feed. After everything, I'm still able to stand and be happy with Yah-Yah and our kids.

Every day I thank God the bullet that hit her went in and out. All of the blood that poured out of the wound made it seem worse than it was. That night she gave birth to our twins. We named our son Yahsari and our daughter Yahsaria. I plan to definitely keep them Y names going. That was six months ago, and we're thriving better than ever. Just looking at my wife and my kids, I know nothing that happened was in vain. It all happened for a reason. Today I married my best friend and soul mate. Yeah, she crazy as hell, but I wouldn't want her any other type of way.

I was in deep thought watching her dance with Thug on the dance floor at our reception. I wanted this big ass wedding, but she didn't. She just wanted to get married in Vegas and have a big reception with the family. Whatever Yah-Yah's spoiled ass wants, she definitely gets.

"I can't believe you went through with it, nephew! I just knew your ass was going to leave that nut at the altar. I lost five bands to my wife betting on this shit!" Malik shook it up with me as he talked his usual shit about Yah-Yah.

"Nah! You should have asked before you threw your money away like that."

"On some real shit though. I'm glad she got a nigga like you. You're exactly what the hell her bi-polar ass needs. I don't think another nigga out here could deal with her ass. Nah, seriously, I know that shit with your family fucked you up. Trust me. I know firsthand how family can be the main ones that fuck you over. Just remember you're one of us now, and we take family serious. Make sure you take care of my niece and them demon seeds because I'm almost positive they are going to take after her." We both laughed and knocked back a shot.

"Uncle Malik, are you over here bothering my husband?" Yah-Yah asked as she came over and kissed me.

"I'm just making sure he straight. Hell, I came over here, and he was looking like that nigga on that movie *Get Out*. Your ass don't got this man in a trance, do you? Where your teacup at crazy ass girl?" We all laughed because this nigga was funny as fuck and played all day.

"I hate you so bad, Uncle Malik."

"On some real shit though Unc is happy for you. Welcome to the family." Malik and I dapped it up after he kissed Yah-Yah on the cheek.

"How are you feeling?" she asked.

"I get to spend the rest of my life with you, so that makes me feel great."

"I just wanted to let you know that I'm so grateful for you. I didn't understand how your love for me would change our lives. Thank you for continuing to love me even on the days that I pushed you away, handling me the way you did made me grow up. Of course, I'm still a spoiled brat, but you've made me become a better woman, wife, and mother. I love you, Yahmeen."

"I love you more."

We kissed, but the sound of a loud bang got our attention. We both stood in shock looking at both Sherita and Gail laid out on the floor. They were dancing on the tables when they collapsed underneath them.

"Oh my god! Why would they be on top of the tables dancing? We're going to lose our damn deposit fucking with them. Are you still sure you want to be a part of this crazy ass family?"

"I'd rather be with you and your crazy ass family any day. I cherish all the madness that comes with them. At least y'all love and accept each other for who you are. I would have loved to have that, but my family wasn't set up that way. Embrace your life, Ka'Jaiyah. You only get one. I'm just happy to be living this life with you and our kids. Fuck the deposit. Let's just enjoy ourselves. After all the bullshit we've been through, we deserve a good time."

After embracing one another, Yah-Yah rushed over to help the rest of the family with Gail and Sherita who were still turnt up. Flashbacks of everything we had been through during our relationship flooded my mind and reminded me of just how hard hood love could be. If you're not strong enough, you'll lose who you love trying to please others. To the world, Yah-Yah didn't deserve me, but in my eyes, she was everything that I needed. Don't no nigga want a boring bitch. She definitely keeps a nigga on his toes. Every gangsta needs a Pit bull in a skirt. I just so happen to be the luckiest nigga in the world because I have just that. Yah-Yah will always be the daughter of a Thug but she's officially the wife of a Gangsta!!!

THE END FOR NOW!!!!

SUBSCRIBE

Text Shan to 22828 to stay up to date with new releases, sneak peeks, contest, and more....

WANT TO BE A PART OF SHAN PRESENTS?

To submit your manuscript to Shan Presents, please send the
first three chapters and synopsis
to submissions@shanpresents.com

COMING TOMORROW

Battle lines are drawn and unfortunately it's the couples that are on the opposite sides. In this twist of events will the ladies choose love or wave their flag in defeat of what's against them? It's the finale of this dope ass love story and what you thought you knew may have been a simple means to an end. It's time for everyone to figure out who and what they want in their lives all while learning about themselves and the lengths the'll go to for love in the process.

COMING 3/3

Katrice is a vibrant 20 year old living in Brooklyn, with her grandmother. Growing up in Marcy projects she has seen it all along with
her best friend Niecey. Trice as she would prefer everyone to call her
had secrets of her own that not even her best friend knew about. The
constant nagging from her grandma rose, was enough to drive her
insane. With nothing to lose she decides it's time for her to break away
and change her environment. She makes up her mind that she needs
freedom, and makes her move to Houston, Texas.

Niecey is the best friend of Trice. They've known each other since
third grade, grew up together in Marcy projects. Niecey has been living
with her mom in Houston for the past 4 years, she works at a call
center downtown and is in love with a street hustler name Juan. She is
definitely ready to paint the town red when her friend touches down
but is she ready to deal with the heartbreak that's coming her way.

Yosari is a local Houston rapper from Cleme Manor fifth ward. The
son of a used to be stay at home mom now turned crack head and a
city worker who was now serving life in prison for murder. He was
raised by his grandmother who also lived in Cleme Manor. Yosari
started writing raps as a freshman in high school. After his best friend
Juan encourages him that he should make a mix tape he figured why

not get his music out there eventually someone will like him. With Juan on the beats and Yosari on the mic he was sure to become a star, but once that fame takes over, he realizes he has no one to share it with or come home to his tenth floor loft in midtown.

Juan was a committed street hustler fresh outta high school. With him being the man of the house he knew he had to step up and help his mom, who was a single mother of three. He was the best friend of local up and coming rapper Yosari, those two were like night and day. Juan wasn't the type to be in the spotlight like Yosari. Yea he knew how to make beats and was the one who made the beats for Yosari's first mixtape, but he had other things on his mind. Juan thought he had it made, money, cars and a bad bitch on his arm, he would want it any other way until a secret of his comes back to haunt him.

CPSIA information can be obtained
at www.ICGtesting.com
Printed in the USA
LVHW092344251019
635428LV00001B/72/P